PRAISE FOR THE HIRING FAIR

Category winner of the 1994 Children's Bisto
Book of the Year Award

"A moving story with a memorable
heroine at its heart."
Madeleine Keane, *Sunday Independent*

"A lovely read..."
Vincent Banville, *The Irish Times*

For Deirdre, Séona,
Iseult and Gráinne Finn

The Hiring
Fair

Elizabeth O' Hara

POOLBEG

Published 2002 by
Poolbeg Press Ltd
123 Grange Hill, Baldoyle
Dublin 13, Ireland
E-mail: poolbeg@poolbeg.com
www.poolbeg.com

© Elizabeth O'Hara 1993

Copyright for typesetting, layout, design
© Poolbeg Press Ltd

1 3 5 7 9 10 8 6 4 2

The moral right of the author has been asserted.

A catalogue record for this book is available from the British Library.

ISBN 1 85371 275 2

Cover illustration by Tom Roche
Cover design by DW Design
Set by Poolbeg Group Services Ltd, in Stone 10/14
Printed and bound by
Cox & Wyman Ltd, Reading, Berkshire.

CONTENTS

1.	Scatterbrain Sally	1
2.	Going to the Céilí	9
3.	Manus	13
4.	After the Funeral	20
5.	The Meitheal	26
6.	Hired!	33
7.	Household Duties	42
8.	Come Sunday	53
9.	A Long Sermon	58
10.	A Visit to Campbells'	63
11.	Divorce!	67
12.	A New Baby	74
13.	Send for the Doctor	83
14.	Pishogues	91
15.	Money to Spend	98
16.	Missing!	103
17.	Lady of the House	111
18.	A Letter	120
19.	Christmas Shopping	125
20.	The Missing Cake	131
21.	Footprints in the Snow!	139
22.	The Intruder Unmasked	145
23.	Happy Christmas!	153
	Glossary	161

Elizabeth O'Hara is the pseudonym of Eilís Ní Dhuibhne, a well-known novelist and short story writer. Her books for children include *The Uncommon Cormorant, Hugo and the Sunshine Girl*, the best-selling Bisto Book of the Year Award Winning *Blaeberry Sunday* and *Penny-farthing Sally*.

1

Scatterbrain Sally

"**S**ally! Get down out of that tree!"

Sally's mother called from the kitchen to her daughter, who was sitting on a high branch of a sycamore tree some yards away from the house. Sally was eating apples and daydreaming, as her gaze wandered over the fields down to the lough. It twinkled like a big roughly cut turquoise in the sunshine. She was thinking how beautiful it looked, and also about how she looked herself: was she beautiful or not beautiful, that was the question. Sometimes she thought one thing, sometimes the other. Sometimes it seemed very important how she looked. Sometimes it seemed quite insignificant. Her thoughts turned to the life she was going to have when she was grown-up. She had plenty of plans. Just at the moment, she felt she would like to be a schoolteacher and to live in a cottage with French windows and a piano in the parlour, like Miss Lynch's, her own teacher. She would drive around in a pony and trap, and eat meringues and éclairs every afternoon for her tea. And maybe after a while she would get married to a rich handsome man, live in a huge house with a river running through the garden and have a carriage and a different dress for every day of the week. Sometimes she thought she would like to live in a bustling city, far away from this remote Donegal glen. She would have a room of her own and would ride a bicycle through the streets, dressed in a flat black hat and a pair of bloomers. At other times, when she was really carried away, she decided to be an explorer. The deep jungles of Africa and the icy wastes of the North Pole awaited her. She would put on a thick tweed skirt and a rucksack and set forth...

"Sally! It's time to peel the potatoes!"

Slowly she climbed down from her green perch and walked across the field towards the house. A flock of rooks which had been having a snack at the foot of the tree scattered as she jumped. Their angry twittering mingled with the sounds of the chickens cackling in the farmyard.

The Gallaghers' house was a long cottage. Its red half-door was flanked on each side by two tiny windows, blinking in the afternoon sunshine. A rambling rose clambered around the door up to the eaves. The roof was of golden thatch, tied down with many strong ropes, to withstand the gales that blew off the Atlantic, winter and summer, at this northernmost tip of Ireland.

Sally crossed the cobbled yard, kicking a lazy goose out of her way, and entered the kitchen. Her mother was at the fire, setting flat loaves against the iron bread stands— "harning stands" they were called, because the oaten bread hardened against them in the heat of the blaze.

"The potatoes are in that bucket, Sally!" she said, the minute Sally walked in. "If you get them peeled I'll make some potato cakes for the tea."

"Oh good!" said Sally, fetching the good knife from the drawer of the dresser, and, standing at the table, she began to work.

"Take one of them bowls, like a good girl, and peel them into it!" ordered her mother, a bit crossly. Sally could be dim sometimes, especially where housework was concerned, although she was quite clever at things you did sitting down, with your head rather than your hands.

Sally sighed very deeply and went back to the dresser. From the selection of painted bowls and plates she chose one large plain brown bowl, suited to potato skins. While she was there she noticed something new.

"Oh, Mother! We've got more jam!"

"Yes, dearie. Hughie the Shop was about while you were over in your tree, and I took one of them jugs from him. We can do with another, I think. And the jam is handy to have, very handy."

"It's lovely, Mother, it really is."

Sally laughed. Her mother had already collected about six of the big blue and red jugs that were given away free with raspberry jam by Hughie the Shop, even though she made plenty of her own jam every year, from blackberries, damsons, rhubarb and wild strawberries—jam that was much tastier than the stuff Hughie had for sale. But she just couldn't resist the enormous, romantic-looking jugs, which made a fine show on her handsome dresser, her pride and joy.

"What's that you're saying? What is it?"

A voice seemed to seep into the kitchen from nowhere, a cracked, crotchety voice.

"We're just talking about the jugs of jam that Hughie the Shop has in his cart, Granny, that's all!" shouted Sally's mother very loudly indeed. She went over to a flowered curtain that hung against the wall at the back of the kitchen and pulled it across. Hidden behind the curtain was a bed and sitting up in the bed was a very old woman whose yellow face was crazed like a pudding bowl and whose skinny body was wrapped in an enormous black fringed shawl.

"Look, there they are on the dresser!"

"Och, yon Hughie's the boyo!" muttered the old woman, with a sour turn to her mouth. "He'll not be long selling you his ware, I'll warrant ye! Hughie would sell his own grandmother, the same Hughie."

"The jugs are free, Granny. They come free with jam."

"Free, is it? I mind the time yon Hughie sold the people back the eggs they were after selling him theirselves for three times the price he gave for them. I do surely. And he has half the parish in the poorhouse with the price of his tay. I'll give ye a half-pound of the best Indian now ma'am and ye can pay me on the slate! Aye, surely. On the slate for the rest of your life. How many people in this parish does that man own, body and soul? How many, I ask ye? The poor damn fools!"

Granny spat on the floor; it was one of her traditional habits. Sally wished she would give it up but it didn't seem likely that she would at her age, which was eighty-one and a half. Having spat two or three times and then cleared her throat for good measure, the old lady took out her pipe and handed it to Mrs Gallagher.

Mrs Gallagher got a burning stick from the fire and reddened the pipe. Then she handed it back to Granny.

"There ye are now, Granny, and don't be bothering us with all that nonsense about Hughie the Shop. Sure isn't the wee man doing his job just like any of the rest of us? The priest tells us not to speak evil of our neighbour."

Granny puffed on her pipe and did not answer.

It was true, as she said, that Hughie the Shop owned half the parish. Mrs Gallagher knew it. Sally knew it. But they didn't want to think about it. There was nothing they could do about it anyway. That was the way things were. Some people were rich and some people were poor and some people were beggars. That was life. You had to put up with it.

At least, that's what Mrs Gallagher believed. Sally wondered. But she didn't bother to wonder very much, since the Gallaghers, luckily, were neither very poor nor rich. They had just about enough of everything. Sally's father, Jack Gallagher, farmed twenty acres of land and did a lot of fishing as well. Mrs Gallagher looked after the three cows and the hens and other fowl. She also did all the baking and cooking, and span and sewed for the whole family. It is true that Sally and her sister, Katie, helped with that. But they did not help a great deal. Sally, at thirteen, was the eldest but she had been born lazy, everyone said. She was happy to believe them and to put up with the name they called her, "Scatterbrain Sally," since it occasionally let her off the hook as far as work was concerned. Little Janey was only three and couldn't do any work at all. Katie, who was eleven, had nimble fingers and did a lot of sewing. Sally didn't. She hated spinning and sewing and knitting as much as she hated all other kinds of housework. What she really wanted to do all the time was read her books. People, like her mother, believed she liked doing schoolwork too, but this was not strictly true. She only did that when she ran out of something to read and in order to avoid doing things around the house and farm. Her main problem in life was not having enough books. Miss Lynch, the schoolteacher she admired so much, lent her one from time to time. She had a big wooden cabinet in her cottage, full of all kinds of delicious volumes. But Sally was a very fast reader and Miss Lynch often forgot to ask her if she wanted a book. So she was often without any at all. Then she made up stories, sometimes just to amuse herself and sometimes for Janey and Katie, who, although thought to be very practical and down to earth, liked nothing as much as a good yarn. Ghost stories were her favourites. Sally knew lots of them. She liked to frighten Katie and Janey, late at night, when the three lay in bed in the same room, with her horrible tales.

Katie came into the kitchen now, just as the discussion about Hughie the Shop was drawing to a close and each of the three women in the house was sinking back into the silence of her own thoughts.

Katie went over to Sally and said, "Need a hand?"

"Oh yes," said Sally, gratefully. She had peeled only two potatoes, and was making slow headway on the third. She handed the knife to Katie and went to the drawer where she fumbled around, pretending to look for another. Katie started to peel the potatoes in the efficient, business-like way which characterised everything she did. Sometimes, looking at Katie performing a simple household task with her hands flying and her face perched primly at a slight angle made Sally want to kick her. She was such a perfectionist. But her mother glanced at her affectionately: Katie was a useful daughter to have around the house. No doubt about that. Whereas Sally! What was going to become of Sally? She was incapable of doing the simplest thing.

"Guess what I heard when I was in the village?" said Katie, suddenly looking up from the basin, which was half-full of neatly peeled potatoes after only about two minutes.

"What?" Sally looked around from the drawer.

"There's going to be a céilí in the school on Sunday. To raise funds for the parish. There'll be tea and scones and apple tart, and dancing from eight until twelve. Everyone is urged to come, as a great time will be had by all."

"Mm, sounds dull," said Sally. "Let's not go. I hate

things that raise funds. They always feel wrong. As if everyone's there only because they've been forced to go, not because they want to."

"Don't be such a spoilsport," said Katie. "You don't have to come if you don't want to. But I do. Can we, Mammy? Please say yes. Please."

"Well...it depends," said her mother in her "we'll see" voice. "How much is it going to cost, Katie? Did you hear that?"

"Threepence a head," said Katie. "It won't break us."

"I suppose not," said Mrs Gallagher. "I have egg money to spare, anyway. Yes, why don't we go? It sounds as if it could be enjoyable. I feel like something enjoyable at the minute."

And she danced a few steps of a slip jig, just to get into the mood of the thing. Katie gave her a disapproving glance: mothers were not supposed to dance, in her opinion. They were past it. Even mothers like Mrs Gallagher, who were young and pretty. But she said nothing and went on working. She finished the potatoes in her usual record time and hung the pot on the crane over the fire: the fireplace was right in the middle of the room; the smoke went out through a small chimney, more of a hole, really, in the middle of the thatch.

"I'm going to wear my new red dress," she announced, firmly, as she backed away from the smoky fire. "I've just crocheted a white collar to go with it. It is beautiful, even if I say so myself. What are you going to wear, Sally?"

"I haven't a clue," said Sally. "I don't think I have anything, come to think of it. I'll just wear what I've on me now. Good enough for that lot at the school anyway."

"You'd have nice dresses just like Katie," said her mother, "if you bothered your head to make them. You can't expect me to spend half my life sewing and making for you, can you? I've enough to do as it is."

And, to confirm her words, she picked up little Janey, who was just about to stick her dirty little fist into the fire after the bread.

Sally sighed and escaped. She liked her family but sometimes being with them made her feel that she was choking. She sneaked out of the kitchen and back to her oak tree. She still had five chapters left in the book Miss Lynch had given her yesterday. *Little Women*, it was called. Sally thought it was the best she'd ever read. But then, she thought that about a lot of books.

2

Going to the Céilí

On Sunday evening, the Gallagher household was hectically busy. There was a queue for the basin on the kitchen table, where everyone wanted to wash their face. Katie was seated on a stool by the window, desperately trying to finish the collar she was sewing for Sally: she couldn't bear to be seen with her sister in her scruffy old pinafore at an important social occasion like the céilí. Mrs Gallagher was rushing in and out, trying to get the cows milked and the hens fed before she went out. Janey flew all over the place, one shoe on and one shoe off, getting in everyone's way.

Only Jack, Sally's father, was calm and indifferent. He sat at the table eating a boiled egg and drinking tea. He was dressed in his old jersey and trousers, and wore a knitted cap. He looked happy, because he was wearing these comfortable old clothes and because he was not going to the céilí. He had thought of a good excuse not to go just in the nick of time. The herring were running in the lough and his plan was to go fishing at dusk with Mickey Russell, his friend and neighbour from down the lane.

"Can you get this out for me, Katie? It's stuck!" Sally

screamed for help from the fireside. She had tied her hair in papers in an effort to make it curl. She'd never done this before but she'd got the idea from the book she was reading. Sally often got ideas from books, and often they did not work quite as well as she would have wished. But she couldn't break the habit. Early in the morning she'd dampened her lank black locks and tied them around twists of brown paper, confident that she would emerge with a cloud of little ringlets later in the day. Now the papers would not come out.

Katie, naturally patient, put down the dress and came to her aid. She pulled and tugged. Sally squealed loudly, trying to avoid her sister's deft but insistent hands. However, in spite of this lack of cooperation Katie managed to get all the papers out in a matter of minutes.

"Oh thank you!" breathed Sally, grateful that the agony was over. "You're such an angel. You've got such clever hands."

"Hm!" Katie, used to such compliments, ignored these and surveyed Sally's head. Some hair flopped down, lank as tow, around her sister's shoulders. Other bits were frizzled like corkscrews and stuck out here and there about her head.

"Well, how do I look?" asked Sally, putting her head coquettishly on one side.

"Why don't you look in the mirror?" said Katie.

Sally crossed the room to the corner where the tiny looking-glass hung, and peered in. She howled in disgust at what she saw.

"I can't go!" she said. "I refuse to go anywhere looking like a...I don't know what! A sheep, or something!"

"Brush it out and see what happens!" said Katie, helpfully handing her the hairbrush which they all shared. Sally brushed disconsolately. After about five minutes, most of the corkscrews had been removed and she was left with a fairly symmetrical puffy bush, standing out on each side of her small face.

"Hm!" she pouted, not altogether disapprovingly, at her reflection. "Now I look more like a collie dog."

"You should have left it alone," Jack spoke from the table. "Your own hair is grand the way it is. You shouldn't interfere with what God gave you."

The Gallagher parents brought God into everything. It was their way. Sally found it embarrassing. As if there was no privacy at all. No matter where you were, God was there, having a look. But she said, "Right as usual, Dad!" and gave him a kiss on the top of his woolly cap. "I wish you were coming with us. Is it really so urgent that you go fishing?"

"Yes it is," he said firmly. "And you'll have a busy day tomorrow, Sally my girl! You'll be salting herrings till the cows come home. We'll put away two barrels, at least; so it'll be all hands on deck."

"Something to look forward to while we dance!" said Katie, with a touch of irony which was unusual for her. She was the sort of girl who never said anything even vaguely funny, as a matter of principle. "Here, Sally, you'll have to manage with this as it is now. I've got to put my own dress on and get ready."

"Thanks, Katie," said Sally, taking the dress with a slightly anxious look. Was it really finished? It was a simple white and black tweed dress, which her mother had made for her. Katie had put on one of the white lace collars she was so good at making. Sally slipped into the room across the hall from the kitchen. She took off the striped pinafore which was her everyday attire, and slid into the new dress. Her bodice and petticoat, both made of white flannel, protected her from the rough texture of the tweed. She tied the skirt at the waist with a sash made of its own cloth, and then put on the matching tweed jacket, which fitted her slim figure like a glove. Finally she brushed her hair again and tied it back with a black ribbon.

When she'd finished dressing she pirouetted around the room. There was no looking-glass here but she didn't need one. She knew that the dress, her first grown-up dress, fitted her like a dream. She felt wonderful!

Back in the kitchen Jack looked up admiringly at her, and said, "You're a fine girl, and no mistake!"

Janey held her hand and said, "You looks nice, Sally!" and her mother cast her an approving glance.

When Katie came in, she looked very pretty, too, in her red dress. But she was not as beautiful as Sally. Her light brown hair and rather pale, watery features were no match for her sister's brown eyes, sallow skin, and raven-black hair. Nevertheless, with Mrs Gallagher in her best black skirt and white blouse, with the new Paisley shawl wrapped around her shoulders, they made a handsome family as they set off for the schoolhouse. Jack stood in the street in front of the house and waved goodbye.

"Wish I could come!" he lied, not very convincingly. "Have fun!"

Janey, in his arms, wept quietly. She wanted to go to the céilí, too, but of course she had to stay at home. Jack would put her to bed and her grandmother would look after her when he went out.

"Don't cry, baby!" Jack whispered to her. "We're going to have a great time, you and me. You'll never guess what I have in my pocket for you!"

Janey stopped crying, and started to search her father's pockets. The rest of the family trotted off down the boreen as quickly as they could.

3

Manus

When they reached the schoolhouse it was already full of people and an old man sometimes known as Paddy the Fiddler and sometimes as Paddy the Belch, because he could fiddle and belch with equal skill, was playing a slow air softly. The dancing had not yet started. People were standing around, drinking cups of tea and eating soda bread and apple tart, and talking. The big room was filled with a huge buzz, which rose above the talking heads like a cloud of bees.

Mrs Gallagher was quickly waylaid by some of her cronies and Katie and Sally searched for their own friends among the throng.

Sally's best friend from school was Maura Canning. She soon spotted her, strategically positioned by the table where the food was laid out, talking to her sister Eileen and her brother Manus. Maura waved and laughed when she saw Sally. Eileen smiled quietly and said hello before rushing off to join some friends. Manus grinned and said nothing. He stood with his back to the table, chewing some bread and staring at the floor. Maura and Sally ignored him completely. They hadn't met for two days and had plenty to chat about. Maura was impressed by Sally's new outfit. She herself was still wearing a pinafore with a white blouse underneath, even though she was quite tall. She gazed enviously at Sally.

"You'll be putting your hair up next!"

"Not before I'm married!" said Sally, laughing.

Manus chewed more furiously than ever and blushed bright pink.

"Which won't be for about a hundred years!" she added.

"If ever!" laughed Maura. Her hair was dramatically red and flowed over her shoulders like a waterfall in the sunset. Sally's, which was tied at the nape of her neck and was still rather puffy, looked more grown-up and discreet.

"Is Miss Lynch here?" asked Sally when they had stopped giggling.

"I saw her when we came in. What do you want her for?"

Maura was slightly jealous of Sally's relationship with their teacher. She knew Sally was not trying to suck up to Miss Lynch but nevertheless she felt excluded from the special and unusual friendship which her friend enjoyed with the glamorous schoolmistress.

"I want to give her back this book she lent me last week," said Sally quickly, well aware of Maura's feelings.

"And get another one, I bet."

"Well, you never know your luck!"

Sally was in luck, as it happened, because just at that moment Miss Lynch approached the two girls and said hello. Sally returned her copy of *Little Women*, which she had been holding carefully wrapped in newspaper.

"You enjoyed it, didn't you?" Miss Lynch asked.

"Yes, I loved it."

"I knew you would. And something told me that you'd have it back this evening. So I brought along another book for you. It's in my basket under my desk. Be sure to get it before you go home, Sally."

"Thank you, Miss Lynch. I will. What is it called?"

"Why don't you wait and see? It'll be a surprise for you!"

At that moment the fiddler broke into a reel, and people began to dance. Sally and Maura went out and joined in the set, which consisted mainly of very young people, like themselves. They whirled and jigged, and by the time the dance was over were pink as carnations and slightly out of breath. They collapsed on one of the benches which had been arranged around the edge of the classroom.

Manus, who had not been dancing, came and sat beside them.

"Lazybones!" teased Maura. "Why didn't you get up and do a step like the rest of us?"

"I'm not much of a dancer," said Manus. His voice had broken recently and sounded very deep and strange to Sally, who remembered him as a little boy. Even though he was two years older than Maura and herself she regarded him as her peer, if not her junior. They had often played Tig and Hide and Seek together, gone swimming from the sheltered little beach down below Sally's house and fished in the burn.

Suddenly she was conscious of his new, adult status. His deep voice was not just strange, it was sonorous and powerful. She cast a sidelong glance at him. He had sandy hair curling lightly over his forehead and ears. His eyes were a clear blue. He had a straight nose and a large mouth, which could laugh loudly and cheerfully—like Maura's— or remain set in a serious line. As it was now. It would be interesting to find out what went on in his head. If anything. As far as Sally could gather, most boys didn't think much. They just tumbled around, getting through school as easily as they could, playing football and thumping one another. But he looked and sounded so different from what he had been when she'd last paid any attention to him that perhaps he might be thinking differently too?

The funny thing was, Sally suddenly became tongue-tied, when she was sitting near him. Her mind went blank in the company of such a big lump of silence. Maura was pattering on about what people were wearing and who had notions about whom. But she couldn't concentrate on that and found it difficult to respond. The problem was finally solved by Manus himself. Making a superhuman effort, he asked Sally to dance.

She followed him woodenly across the floor and was led into a fast-moving set. The dancing was more energetic and athletic than any field sport, and it wasn't possible to do it and feel nervous at the same time. Sally and Manus jumped and whirled, like all the other couples, and swung as fast as they possibly could when their turn came to do a swing. Girls usually liked swinging because it was almost the only opportunity they got actually to feel their partner's arm around their waist. But the romantic bit lasted for only about half a second. Then the object of the exercise was to swing so fast that one or other partner would fall down from an attack of dizziness. Sally and Manus were quite fast swingers but neither of them managed to collapse: the unspoken rule was that you had to be really compelled to drop. Faking was looked down upon.

The great advantage of set-dancing, as far as boys were concerned, was that there was no need to talk to girls while you were doing it. The only requirement was physical fitness. Manus was known as a good footballer and runner. He had what it took to dance very well. Sally had about five dances with him, but they hardly talked to one another at all. So she didn't find out what was going on inside his head, although she became very familiar with the way his feet worked. Oh well, it was a start, she supposed.

At midnight, Mrs Gallagher, who had had a lovely time chatting with her friends, rounded up Sally and Katie, saying it was time to go home. Sally said goodbye quickly to Manus, and then to Maura.

"Manus likes you," Maura said, staring her in the eye.

"Does he?" asked Sally, and dashed off, feeling very confused, without waiting for a reply.

Although she was feeling tired out, she did not forget to go to Miss Lynch's basket and fetch the promised book. There it was, in a dark blue cover, lying on top of the big wicker basket. Sally grabbed it and glanced at the title, before tucking it under her shawl for safekeeping on the way home. _Uncle Tom's Cabin_ was the name of the book. She'd never heard of it before.

Mrs Gallagher, Katie and Sally walked home more slowly than they had come to the céilí. The sky was a deep navy blue, cloudy but with some stars visible. There was a half-moon tossing among the clouds and they could just make out the shape of the hills, the trees and the hedgerows. Wind whistled and shivered through the trees. Occasionally they heard some animal stirring in the ditch, and when they passed Packy Doherty's cornfield the corncrake croaked.

The three walked in silence. They were tired, glad to feel the cool night air brushing against their skin after the heat of the schoolhouse and busy with their own thoughts. The even rhythm of their walking soothed those thoughts, as the air cooled their hot bodies. Sally was in a state of shock. "Manus likes you." No boy had ever liked her before. She had never expected that any would. In fact, she had never given the matter a moment's thought. She knew boys liked girls of course, and vice versa. But it hadn't seemed like something that would affect her, not for a long time anyway. Now this was happening to her, before she had had a chance to think about it. A boy liked her. What was she supposed to do about that?

Maybe Maura was wrong?

When they reached the house, it was in darkness. The dying embers of the fire glowed in the kitchen, and from her bed in the corner the slow, heavy breathing of Granny could be heard.

"All asleep!" said Mrs Gallagher quietly. "Off to bed now, the pair of you, and don't wake Janey or Daddy!"

"No, Mother!" they said in sleepy unison. And, kissing their mother goodnight, they went up to the loft, where they shared a bed with Janey. Mrs Gallagher left the kitchen to go to her own bedroom at the other side of the room.

Sally and Katie were already undressed and lying down when they heard their mother returning. She came to the foot of the ladder leading to their loft and said, in a loud whisper:

"Daddy hasn't come home yet!"

Sally stirred uneasily. Daddy's fishing trips almost always finished before midnight, sometimes well before. It was not like him to be this late. Still, the herring were plentiful so he might have stayed to get an extra large catch.

"He'll be along soon, Mother," she said. "He's probably just getting as many herrings as he can, to keep us busy for weeks."

"It's not such a bad night," said Katie sleepily. "He's bound to be all right, Mother. Don't worry. Go to bed and get some sleep. He'll be back when you wake up."

But when the early crowing of the cockerel wakened the

Gallaghers the following morning, Jack Gallagher was not in his bed, but lying in the seaweed at the bottom of the clear green water in the bay.

4

After the Funeral

Nobody ever did find out what exactly had happened to Jack Gallagher. He had gone out fishing alone: when he called on his friend Mickey Russell, Mickey had not been feeling well, and didn't go with him. It had been a windy night, but Jack had survived worse before. Some people suggested that he had had some sort of attack, a fainting fit or a heart attack, while he was at sea, and had lost control of the boat. The Gallaghers found this hard to believe, since he had never been sick in his life. But it seemed the most likely explanation.

The tragedy affected the family gradually. At first the blow was softened by the demands of the wake and funeral, even though Jack's was a sombre wake. Nobody wanted to dance or sing or play rowdy party games at his vigil, as they would have if an old person whose death had been expected had died.

"It's me that should be lying there, not him!" muttered Granny, angrily rather than sadly, through her tears. Jack had not been her son but she had loved him very much. Everyone loved him because he had been so cheerful and courageous.

When the funeral was over and the common routine of life was restored, the Gallaghers felt their loss more deeply and they had the greatest difficulty in coming to terms with the fact that he was dead. It was impossible to believe that he was no longer with them: their good-humoured father, the lynchpin of the scatty, boisterous family. Sally still expected to see him standing in the field behind the horse, or wielding the scythe in the corn with strong even rhythms that soothed one just to look at them, when she left the house to go to school in the mornings. When she came in at dinnertime, it was always a new blow to see his empty place at the table. He had been quiet, but so steady, so important—the rock on which the family life was built. Above all, he had seemed so indestructible.

Katie reacted to the loss with silent stoicism. Always rather quiet, she hardly uttered a word for weeks, but went about her work, doing her best to keep the home running as efficiently and comfortably as ever. She felt her father's death deeply: of the three girls, she was the one who least resembled him in looks and character. When he had been alive they had seemed to have a less lively relationship than that enjoyed by either of the other two girls with him, but, although they had exchanged few words, there had been a special bond between them, arising, perhaps, out of the difference in character.

It was fortunate for the Gallaghers that Katie reacted as she did, because without her the house would have stopped functioning. Janey, of course, was too young to understand what had happened. Sally was too dreamy and impractical to be useful in an emergency, which is what the situation was: she mooned around, sentimentally recalling her beloved father and crying sporadically. She also had a new problem, which she found puzzling and inappropriate at a time like this. Just a few days after the funeral was over, she suddenly found herself thinking about Manus. She just woke up one morning and he was on her mind, and would not get out of it. It was very strange, at first, and then irritating. An ordinary boy who was just moderately good at school, who spent his time hunting rabbits and fishing. She'd never given him a thought. Now he took over her mind, completely, for two or three days, when she should have been thinking of other things. But there was nothing she could do about it. For three days, she daydreamed, envisaging various situations in which they were alone together: on the beach, up in the mountains, or in a boat. She imagined she was struck down by a serious illness. She was lying in bed for weeks, unable to open her eyes. Then Manus came to see her, to say goodbye. And she opened her eyes slowly and smiled at him. Or she imagined that she was the one who saved him from danger. That he was drowning and she rescued him, or pulled him away from the path of a bull just in the nick of time. He would say, "That was a close shave! You saved my life," and be eternally grateful to her.

The only time she actually saw him in the flesh was at Mass. And then the only bit of him she saw was the back of his head, for about five seconds, while she was walking past the pew at the very back of the chapel, where he always sat. She was on her way up to the middle, Mrs Gallagher's favourite position. Occasionally, if she was very lucky, she would catch a glimpse of his whole face on her way out. By then he would be outside, leaning against the wall on the road opposite the chapel with the other boys. She would look very quickly, just long enough to ascertain that he was there and to refresh her mental picture of him, and then look away again. Of course they never acknowledged one another, or spoke. That would have been impossible, with all the other boys, and other people in general, hanging around. And besides, he would be embarrassed by Sally because her father had died. She knew that. She had noticed how other people reacted. Some of her friends, most of them, didn't know what to say to her about it. They gave her funny looks. They were kind, but it was clear that they thought she was a bit of a freak, a girl without a father, a girl whose father had drowned. At least they thought that for a while. Then they got used to it or forgot about it. But Manus wouldn't forget, since he had never spoken to her since Jack's death. Every time he saw her it must be the thing that jumped into his head.

The person most affected by the drowning was, of course, Mrs Gallagher. She made courageous attempts to keep the sadness and resentment she felt under control. She felt a terrible mixture of loneliness and anger. What had she done to deserve such bad luck? It seemed so stupid and unfair. Fortunately she was kept so busy that she didn't have time to give in to self-pity. Janey and her old mother required as much attention as before and demanded it if they didn't get it. Poor Mrs Gallagher attended to them as best she could, and did her best to be the loving, caring homemaker she always had been. But her efforts failed from time to time. Katie or Sally would come upon her, sitting with the potato knife or the kneading board on her lap, staring into space like a wounded rabbit. And indeed that is what she felt like: Jack's absence was like the loss of a limb to her. She felt that she had been cut in half, like an apple, and that she was constantly trying to find the part that was missing.

But time helped her, and everyone else. As the summer moved on, they became accustomed to what had happened and by September, life was restored to some sort of normality. This was partly thanks to Katie's efforts. She behaved like a person twice her age. She had begun to take responsibility for the chickens and the cows, and had persuaded Sally to help her harvest the blackcurrants and gooseberries. Mrs Gallagher, gradually emerging from her state of numb shock, had mechanically made jam, as she was accustomed to do every August. Little Janey and Granny had helped with that, putting muslin lids on the jars and tying them down.

As to the farmwork, the neighbours rallied round and formed a gathering, what they called a "meitheal," to harvest the potatoes, cut the hay, and bring in a load of turf from the bog for the Gallaghers. Later, when they had time to spare from their own chores, there would be another meitheal to do the thrashing. The day of the meitheal was the most pleasant and exciting event the household had enjoyed since the drowning. The farm and kitchen were a hive of activity. Katie and her mother were busy all day, preparing food for the men and boys who were working for them in the fields. They made huge loaves of soda bread, to be eaten with butter and jam and tea in the late afternoon; they cooked cauldrons of mashed potatoes; they baked potato cakes and apple pies. Sally gathered blackberries, which they would eat with cream. She worked her way along the edge of the golden fields, pulling the plump purple berries from the brambles and dropping them into a wooden bucket. The bees buzzed, the red admirals fluttered across the fragrant hedges. The sun burned her already brown arms and legs. She felt happy, really happy, for the first time since Jack had died.

Her excitement was increased by the knowledge that one of those who would eat the blackberries was Manus. He was out in the fields, part of the meitheal of good neighbours who were helping the Gallaghers. If this were a normal meitheal and not one for a recently bereaved family, it would end with a great party. The dancing and singing would go on far into the night. That would not happen this time. Nevertheless, there would be a good dinner and the men would stay and smoke their pipes, and perhaps someone would tell a story. That would not be considered too boisterous. Manus might stay on, perhaps until it was quite late. He might be in her kitchen. He might talk to her! This thought made her both very nervous and very happy.

5

The Meitheal

When the day's work was over, the group of ten or so men and boys washed their hands and faces in the tub that had been left outside the door for this purpose, and came into the kitchen. Katie and Mrs Gallagher, helped by neighbouring women who had come to give them a hand, had pulled out the table and laid it with their best ware. There were jugs of milk and cream, platters of buttered bread, bowls of jam and blackberries, already waiting for the guests when they arrived. They were immediately served with huge plates of potatoes and salted herrings. The men fell to with hearty appetites. You would think they hadn't eaten in a week. Most of them put away about ten big potatoes, before they started on the other food, which they regarded as a little extra flavouring, hardly worth bothering about. When they had finally stuffed themselves to capacity, about an hour after the meal had begun, the table was cleared and pushed out of the way. Then the men, as Sally had predicted, stretched their legs and lit their pipes. They were in no hurry to go home. This was their favourite time, the hour after dinner, when their bodies thawed and relaxed after the hard labour of the day, when their stomachs were full and their minds easy and smooth as the golden corn that lay in sheaves in the Gallaghers' fields. For more than twelve hours they had worked together, unable to spare the time or energy for more than the bare necessities of conversation. Now they felt an urge to be entertained.

There was no singing or music. Nobody expected that. But, sure enough, after an hour or so of small talk, one of the older men named Skinny Joe, in spite of, or perhaps because of, the fact that he weighed about seventeen stones, began to tell a long story. Everyone knew the story, and had heard it many times before. But hardly anyone could tell it as well as Skinny Joe and it was considered a special treat to hear him perform. The story was about a boy who was thrown out of home and went wandering around the world. Eventually he rescued a princess from a dragon and, after some further adventures, married her and became a rich man.

"And if there's a lie in that story do not blame me," Joe finished up his long, long tale. "Because it was not I who made it up or composed it."

Sally sat at the corner of the kitchen nearest the door, and listened. Manus was, as she had hoped, in the kitchen too, but at the other end of it, locked in by a group of men and boys. It seemed highly unlikely that she would manage to break through their guard and get a chance to talk to him. This irritated her at first, so that she could not concentrate on the story. But after a few minutes she was transported by the music of Joe's voice and words to the far-off, wonderful land where the princess lived. She saw, as the episodes of the tale unfolded, the city with its marble spires, the high turreted walls, the dark gloomy cave to which the dragon took his victims. The voice of the storyteller rose and fell like the flames flickering on the hearth, speeding up when the action became exciting, slowing down when grave matters were being dealt with. Her heart rose and fell with his tones: one moment hopeful and optimistic, the next in the depths of despair. She was far from her kitchen, far from the house. All the details of her own life were forgotten, as she lived the adventures of the fairy-tale.

As it finally drew to a close, Joe's voice grew soft and gentle. He almost whispered the final lines. It was as if he, too, were reluctant to leave the magic world he had been describing and return to mundane existence. For a few minutes after he had finished talking, nobody spoke. Each member of the audience kept peace with himself or herself, gazing into the glowing fire as if into another world. Or into their own hearts and souls.

During this quiet interlude, when time seemed to stand still and be poised between one dimension and another, Sally got up and went out of the hot room into the farmyard. She sat on a big stone that was placed outside the door, and let the cool breeze cool her face. It was a lovely night: mild, with the faintest wind. The sycamore trees beside the byre whispered; the lough gleamed, darkest blue below the shadowy fields. It was very still but behind the silence was the brightly lit house, full of the muffled sound of happy voices.

"This is the best time we've had since Daddy died," Sally was thinking. That had seemed like the worst thing that could possibly happen. It had seemed like something that they would never get over. But today had been a wonderful day. The sun had shone, the blackberries had been ripe. All the Gallaghers, even Sally's mother, had been busy and happy. And now their house, the tragic house, was filled with people who were enjoying themselves. It was full of happiness. Life was surprising. "Sometimes up, sometimes down," as one of the proverbs Granny was so fond of spouting out at all times expressed it.

When she had been sitting there, thinking, for about ten minutes, she heard footsteps.

"Hello," Manus said. "What are you doing out here on your own?"

Sally looked up in surprise. She had never heard him say such a long sentence before.

"Oh, just cooling off a bit. It's so hot in there."

"How are you?"

"I'm all right. How are you?"

"OK. I notice you are not at school these days."

"No. Mammy wanted us to stay at home this week, because of the work today. We'll be going back again on Monday, I suppose. What is happening there?"

"You know, the usual…"

They talked for about half an hour, and then they went back into the kitchen together, to get some tea. Sally had never felt a conversation move so fast, and be so engrossing. It was better than reading a book!

The next day brought a bombshell for Katie and Sally, a bombshell almost more shocking than the news of their father's death.

They were seated at the breakfast table. Janey was trying to eat a boiled egg, and having problems: her face was streaked with yellow yolk. Katie came to her little sister's aid. Sally, meantime, was helping herself to bread and jam.

"School again next week!" she said.

Something in her mother's attitude to the question of school had made Sally feel uneasy. She hadn't wanted to stay away this week, but had done so because Mrs Gallagher had insisted. Now she wanted to have the whole question cleared up.

Mrs Gallagher looked up from her tea. "Yes," she said, with a deep sigh. "Yes."

She didn't say anything else for a while. Her eyes glazed over, as they sometimes did nowadays.

"What is it, Mother?" Katie asked. "Is something wrong?"

"Is something wrong?" her mother repeated, in a bland, expressionless tone. "Is something wrong?"

Suddenly her face reddened and when she spoke again her voice was angry. "Of course there's something wrong, you little fool! Of course there is. Your father's dead; or hadn't you noticed? Your father's dead, there's nobody to look after the farm, we've no money to pay the rent and it's only a matter of time till we're thrown out of here and on to the parish."

Katie turned her head away and concentrated on feeding Janey, who looked as if she was going to start screaming.

Sally felt her own volatile temper flare up.

"That's not fair, Mother. Katie just wants to help. And I don't see what the problem is: we got a lot of help yesterday, the farm seems to be going fine."

"Musha God help you, if that's what you think," said her mother, her voice calm again, but not exactly cheerful. "We can get by for another month or two, sure enough. But what's going to happen then? We can't rely on the neighbours forever. And nobody's going to go fishing for us, or go hunting, or go making furniture and building houses around the countryside."

Jack Gallagher had been a carpenter as well as a fisherman, and had earned some extra money doing odd jobs in the neighbourhood.

"The problem is, girls," went on Mrs Gallagher, quite

controlled and matter-of-fact now, "that we have no way of making money. If it were just a question of food we'd survive. But it's not. We still pay rent to Mr Betts, in spite of all the efforts of the Land League. Until we own our own farm we'll have to do that. And we need money to pay rent. If we lose this farm, what have we? What are we?"

"Miss Lynch says that in a few years, thanks to Parnell, we'll all be able to buy our farms."

Parnell was a famous politician, the leader of the Irish Party at Westminster. He was working on laws which would help Irish tenants to get possession of the farms they now rented, and also for Home Rule for Ireland. Everyone had high hopes of him.

"Yes, that's what they all say. But it's not happened yet, not here. And in the meantime we have old Betts and his agent with their hands out every six months, demanding the rent. The first of November is gale day still, in spite of Parnell. And I haven't got the rent. We'll be evicted."

Katie and Sally looked anxious. Even Janey stopped howling and her face took on a serious expression. Already she knew what the word "evicted" meant.

"What can we do?" asked Katie.

Sally wished she hadn't asked. Because she knew, deep in her heart, in the place where the most terrible fears are hidden, what the answer would be.

"There is only one thing we can do. It breaks my heart," said Mrs Gallagher. Her voice was very even. "You girls will have to go to work. You'll have to go to the hiring fair in Milford at the end of October and be hired out. That's the only way I can get the rent money in time. You can go to school for the time being but come the hiring fair you'll have to give it up."

Katie looked very glum.

Sally cried, "The hiring fair? But that's slavery! It's like *Uncle Tom's Cabin*! We can't go to the hiring fair, Mother! We can't!"

Her mother got up and left the table without saying another word.

6

Hired!

The third of November was a bleak, blustery day. All over the square of the small town of Milford, children and their parents huddled together for shelter from the north-east wind that whistled through the lanes and alleys. It whipped at Sally's ears and chin and nose, turning them purple with cold.

She and Katie stood with their mother on the pavement outside Diamond's public house. They had said goodbye to Janey at home, trying to hide from her the fact that they would not see her again for six months. That this year, they would not be at home to see what Father Christmas brought her, or to bring her sliding on the frozen lake in the middle of the mountains during the cold spell that always came in January. They pretended that they were going to Milford to shop at the fair. This was not exactly tactful, because Janey wanted to go too. Shopping was her favourite activity. The word "fair" filled her mind with the taste of sweets, to which she was helplessly addicted, and with visions of toys, which she hardly ever got, but which she loved. It was enough to make anyone scream, the thought of missing all that. And she did scream, and howl, and dance up and down on the floor. In the end the neighbour who had come to look after her had to pin her down on her lap and ask her own son to guard the door while Sally and Katie and their mother made their escape. The last sound in their ears as they left home was the sound of their little sister's screams of frustration, mixed up with Granny's grunts from the bed and the cackling of the hens.

And now, the hiring fair. It was not amusing, at least, not in the sense that Janey anticipated. What was for sale were not sweets and toys, but men, women and children. Half the people who were crowding the big grey square were waiting to be "hired": that is, they wanted to be employed by farmers from Tyrone and Derry, or from farther afield, for the next six months. They would sell their services for a few pounds, say goodbye to their homes and friends, and set off to live and work among strangers. In many instances, they would not know what to expect in their new places of employment. They might be well or badly treated. The next six months might be heaven or hell. Only one thing was certain: they were going to be far away from everything and everyone they knew best. For the six months, to all intents and purposes they would be owned by the farmers who would hire them today.

Many of the people waiting to be hired were children, some of them much younger than Sally and Katie. A boy standing next to them with his father and mother looked about seven years old, and some of the other children were not much older. Sally, at thirteen, and Katie at eleven, were among the biggest children in the square: "children," because Mrs Gallagher had dressed them in their pinafores and black stockings, to emphasise their youth. Their new grown-up frocks were packed in the little baskets that lay at their feet. "Only for Sundays!" their mother had admonished, wagging her finger. But the real reason she asked them to wear their pinafores was that she wanted them to be treated as children and not as adults by their new bosses. Even though they would earn more money as grown-ups, they would have to work harder for it. She thought it was all hard enough as it was.

It was only nine o'clock. The Gallaghers had set off from home before six. One of their neighbours, Paddy Friel, had given them a ride in his donkey and cart half-way to the town and they had walked the rest of the way, a distance of about four miles. It had been a slow, painful journey, with the wind and rain slapping against their faces and their bags weighing down their backs.

Sally patted her basket, trying to get some comfort from it. Inside there was a change of underwear, two nightdresses and her Sunday frock and shoes. Besides, she had packed a jotter and pencil, and her copy of _Uncle Tom's Cabin_. She had already read the latter, but had enjoyed it so much and spoken of it in such glowing terms that Miss Lynch had presented it to her before she left home. She did not say what she was thinking: that there might not be many books in the place Sally was going to. But Sally guessed her thoughts: the same idea had already occurred to her, although she was hoping for the best. After all, you never knew your luck! Miss Lynch had hugged Sally then, and told her to be brave.

It had only been yesterday. Already it seemed a lifetime away. Thousands of miles from this awful place, where farmers were already marching purposefully around, looking prospective servants up and down, pinching their muscles and feeling their bones to test their strength. It was too like the slave markets described in the book Sally had in her bag—and in her head—to be palatable.

A large man wearing knee breeches and a black three-cornered hat came up to Mrs Gallagher and asked her if the girls were hers.

"Are they your weans?" was what he said, actually. Sally understood what he said, but with difficulty: she was not used to hearing English spoken except by children and the teacher, in school. Irish was the language all ordinary grown-ups spoke at home.

Mrs Gallagher nodded, unable to speak in the first shock of experiencing what she had been dreading for weeks.

"Stand out here, you!" he pointed at Katie with his stick.

Katie, ever obedient, stepped meekly forward.

He looked her up and down, then walked around and examined her from the back. His face was red and there was a big mole on his chin with tufts of red wiry hair growing out of it. On his breath was the unmistakable smell of whiskey: most of the farmers in Milford smelt of it, since the public houses opened early especially for the fair.

"Not a bad wee lassie!" he said, his examination over. Sally breathed a sigh of relief on Katie's behalf. At least she was not going to be pinched or measured, as some of the children were.

Mrs Gallagher had by now picked up enough courage to look him in the eye.

"Aye, Mam, she's a fine wean. How much are you looking for her?"

"Four pounds," said Mrs Gallagher in a surprisingly firm tone.

The man scratched his head, lifting his cap slightly in order to get at the itchiest bits.

"There's them that cost less," he said after a few moments' happy scratching.

Mrs Gallagher said absolutely nothing. Sally and Katie

watched, spellbound by this interplay. They had hardly ever heard their mother speak English, or display such confidence. Where had she got it from? If she was putting on an act, it was certainly a convincing one. So engrossed were they in her performance, if that's what it was, that for a moment they forgot that it was Katie who was the object of the bargaining.

"Of course, she's a fine lassie, and a good worker, I'll be bound."

Mrs Gallagher spoke: "She's one of the best workers going. She can milk and churn. She can spin and sew and dye and knit. She can bake bread and wash clothes and look after children better than most women twice her age."

"Hm!" the man scratched his head again, but in a business-like, not a thoughtful, way this time. "I believe you!" he said with a grin. "I'll take her, even at four pounds! Them that buys cheap buys dear, my mother always says, and it's my mother who's paying for her."

Mrs Gallagher stood her ground. Oddly enough, in spite of the horror with which they had viewed the proceedings, all the Gallaghers were pleased that the man had reached this decision and was happy to pay more than the going rate for Katie. It confirmed their belief that they were better than the run of the mill. Besides, it meant that Mrs Gallagher would already have enough money to pay the rent next time it was due, although she'd be in arrears until then.

"There is a condition!" said Mrs Gallagher.

"What's that?" he asked, taken aback. One did not expect conditions from the likes of these people, especially not when they'd already driven a hard bargain.

"This is the first time these girls have been away from home. I want both of them to be hired in the same **neighbourhood.**"

"Begob, madam, that is easier said than done!" said the man, with a disbelieving laugh. "I need one maid, not half a dozen!"

"If you can't arrange for the other girl to go with her sister, you can't have either of them," said Mrs Gallagher.

"It's all right, Mother," Katie began to say.

Mrs Gallagher stopped her.

"No, Katie, it's not all right. We'll do it this way. It will work, you mark my words. I'll not have you going off all alone. That's the least I can do for you!"

The farmer was still looking at Katie, and from her to Sally. Finally he said, "I'll see what I can do. There's a neighbour of mine about the place somewhere, William Stewart by name. There's a chance he might take the other wee lass, although I know for a fact it's a grown woman he's looking for."

"Ask him if he's interested," said Mrs Gallagher. "We'll stay here. If you're not back in half an hour we'll take it that you're not interested."

The man smiled to himself and went off. They watched him cross the square and look around. Soon he disappeared into a pub.

"The last we'll see of him, probably!" said Mrs Gallagher. "But don't you worry, there'll be others."

They had to wait for half an hour before going on the market again. During that time, several men came up and looked at the girls with interest. Mrs Gallagher told them all to come back after ten o'clock.

"The best ones are always gone!" said one of the farmers, an exceptionally tall man, with a confident air and a handsome face. Sally wished she could go to work for him, but when she mentioned this to her mother she said, "He's the last one I'd hire you to. He looks like a conceited pup."

Sally stared at the young farmer as he strode majestically through the throng. His eyes glistened, and so did his boots. He was the most smartly dressed farmer at the fair. But he did, as Mrs Gallagher said, look a bit stuck up. His expression, as he examined the people up for hire, was haughty.

The little boy next to them, whose name, they had learned by listening, was Johnny, was looked over by many farmers and rejected by all of them as being too small. Johnny and his parents became increasingly dismayed, and Sally, although she secretly hoped that Johnny would not be employed, since he looked much too young to have to leave his parents, felt sorry for them. In the end a big rough farmer wearing thick tweeds came and examined Johnny minutely. He asked Johnny what age he was and Johnny said, "Ten."

"Small for your age," the farmer said suspiciously.

"You can have him for three pounds, sir," said Johnny's father, a small thin man with a scabby face. "He's a grand wee worker, a great lad."

"He's small," said the farmer. "Here, young fellow, can you lift that?"

And he threw a large sack of potatoes at Johnny's feet.

Making an enormous effort, Johnny hoisted it onto his shoulders. Sally and Katie could see that he almost burst with the attempt and began to hate his parents, especially his father, who had a weak, whining voice. Sally hoped against hope that the farmer would not take him.

But he did. Johnny, however small, was cheap at three pounds. A bargain offer. The last they saw of him was him running along beside the horse of the farmer, carrying a heavy bag and crying his eyes out. Tears came to their own eyes, looking at him. His own parents did not see: they had left the marketplace as soon as the bargain was made, and had gone into one of the public houses.

The Gallaghers sat glumly on their baskets for some time after this, trying to forget the picture of poor little Johnny running for all he was worth alongside the fat farmer on his horse.

"Maybe he has a kind wife," said Sally, finally, with an attempt at optimism.

"He doesn't look like a man who has a kind wife!" said Katie.

"You wouldn't know," said Mrs Gallagher. "Kind women often marry the most awful men. It is a thing I've noticed."

At that moment, the man who had spoken with them earlier returned, bringing with him his friend—none other than the farmer Sally had admired.

"This is William Stewart," said the farmer. "And my own name, by the way, is Robert Campbell. Willie here has agreed to take on the big girl, and I'll take the wee one."

"Her name is Katie. Katie Gallagher. And the big girl is Sally."

"Aye. Katie. I'll take Katie here. It's a companion for me ould mother I'm looking for to tell ye the truth. She's getting on and she needs a nice wee girl to help her around the house and so on, ye know what I mean?"

Now that he had decided on hiring Katie, Mr Campbell was much more talkative than hitherto. He seemed to be regarding the Gallaghers almost as equals.

"And what does Mr Stewart want?" asked Mrs Gallagher, suspiciously.

"Och, just a girl about the house and byre, you know. My wife could do with someone to give her a hand in the dairy. And with the weans."

"How many children have you?" asked Mrs Gallagher,

in a less suspicious tone.

"We've three now, madam, and a fourth on the way. We'll be needing a hand then too."

Robert Campbell went on to explain that he and William Stewart lived less than half a mile from one another, in a village called Ballygowl, in Tyrone.

"No need to worry about your girls, ma'am," he went on. "They'll be well looked after with us, never you fear. And they'll be sent back here on the thirtieth of April, safe and sound. Never you worry about them."

"All right," said Mrs Gallagher finally. "They can go."

"Don't worry about them, ma'am," said Mr Campbell, a kind note coming into his husky voice. "They'll be all right. We'll treat them well enough."

"They're good girls," said Mrs Gallagher. But her voice let her down. She couldn't say anything more. Tears streamed down her cheeks as she hugged Sally and Katie and watched them set off with their new employers. She felt even sadder than she had when Jack had drowned.

7

Household Duties

The journey to Ballygowl lasted the whole day. The girls, however, were luckier than most children going on hire. They did not have to travel on foot but rode with their employers in a horse and cart; Campbell and Stewart had shared one for the purpose of this trip. As well as the human passengers there were three pigs in the back of the cart, sharing quarters with Sally and Katie. The men sat on the box in front.

The cart was not the most comfortable of vehicles. But, once she had made friends with the pigs and grown accustomed to their stench, Sally began to enjoy herself. In spite of her deep distaste for the idea of going on hire, and in spite of her constant reminders to herself that she was now no better off than a slave, she could not suppress a rising, bubbling sense of adventure. Always fascinated by the prospect of travel, she had never before been further than a town called Buncrana, which was on the far side of the lough from her own home. And that had been once only, long ago, when her father had given in to her entreaties that he should take her fishing with him. Most of her long trips had been to the town closest to home, only five miles distant. That had seemed far enough. But now here she was, setting out on a long journey, to a place where nobody in her family had ever been before! As the rugged coastal landscape gave way to small level fields of green grass, as the low heather-covered hills of Donegal vanished behind her and the high blue mountains of Tyrone came into view on the horizon, she forgot her fear of the future, and began to relish the present experience thoroughly.

Katie was not so quick to let go of her forebodings. She had a less adaptable character than Sally's and would not have been inclined to accept change under any circumstances. But she could not but feel that fate had dealt Sally the better hand (Sally felt this too, although of course she could not admit it to Katie). Robert Campbell, the evidence so far suggested, was a trustworthy, even a kind, man. But he was not interesting or handsome. A man with a cap like his, and trousers tied at the knee with a thick piece of string, could not live in a very attractive house. Could he? Moreover, the thought of his aged mother to whom she would have to play the lady's maid did not attract her in the least. She envied Sally the prospect of a young handsome couple as her employers, and the company of a houseful of young children.

"I'll probably have my hands full!" whispered Sally, when Katie voiced some of her misgivings. "All those children!"

"I hope you can handle them," said Katie unkindly, remembering Sally's clumsiness in her own home. "Maybe we should exchange jobs?"

Sally just laughed and pinched the fattest pig, who squealed violently in response.

Night had fallen hours before they reached their destination. The girls were sleepy and cold, kept awake only by the jolting of the cart, when at last it drew to a halt at the roadside, beside a high black hedge. Robert Campbell dismounted and said to Katie: "We're home, girl. Get down now."

Sally opened her sticky eyes and saw through a gap in the bushes the outline of a long, low house, not unlike her own house in appearance but twice the size. It had a thatched roof, like theirs, and appeared to have white walls. But in front instead of a yard was a garden, fenced in with a high hedge and full of shadowy, whispering trees. There was no light in the house and in the dark night it looked gloomy.

Katie took her basket and stepped slowly out of the cart.

"Goodbye! Goodbye, Kate!" said Sally, giving her a tight hug. Tears sprang to her eyes: she was tired and anxious now. This final parting was, somewhat to her surprise, the hardest to bear. She and Katie had often seemed to be rivals, and had frequently quarrelled with one another. But at this moment Sally felt that she loved Katie more than anyone in the world.

Katie herself could not speak at all. She felt more tired and drained than she ever had before. She had been so much a part of her home that, separated from it, she felt as if she hardly existed. She squeezed her sister desperately.

"We'll probably see each other very soon!" whispered Sally. "Take care, take care!"

"Come on, now, girl," said Campbell impatiently. "It's very late."

Sally wished he would call her sister by her name, and not address her as "Girl!"

The sisters loosened their embrace and reluctantly separated. William Stewart shouted at the horse and the cart rumbled off. Sally watched Katie follow Campbell up the narrow path and go into the house.

Within ten minutes she was being hustled into the Stewarts' house. Too exhausted to take note of her surroundings, she pulled off her outer garments and tumbled into a bed. Any bed would have been welcome at that moment, but she was just alert enough to notice that it was as clean and comfortable as her own bed at home. In seconds she was sound asleep.

The sound of a child crying awakened her. For a moment she believed she was at home and that the cry was Janey's. Then she looked around. She was in a very tiny room, all by herself. A small window over the bed admitted a long bar of brilliant yellow sunlight, which made a pathway through the air along the length of the bed and down to the door at its foot. Voices from below told her that she was upstairs somewhere and also that the rest of the household had got up. She had no idea of the time: at home, she was always guided by the crowing of the cockerel (time to get up) or by the height of the sun or the strength of the light. It was not so easy to judge these signals in a strange place. Nevertheless, she guessed it was high time to be out of bed and speedily left it.

Quietly she slipped out of her room, and walked downstairs. The stairs led directly into the kitchen. Halfway down the stairs Sally paused and observed the scene below. The room she saw was twice as big as the kitchen at home. It was painted white. There was a big brick hearth instead of a central fireplace. Opposite the hearth was an enormous dresser, filled with an assortment of delph and china ware that would have been the envy of Mrs Gallagher. One wall was lined with large chests, painted dark blue and decorated with illustrations of flowers. In the middle of the floor, itself tiled in a black-and-white chequered pattern, was a long wooden table around which the Stewart family was gathered.

Mrs Stewart caught sight of Sally standing on the stairs and said, "You must be Sally! Come down and meet us all!"

She had a soft pleasant voice. Her face was soft, too, and beneath her frilled white cap her hair was smooth and fair. She was dressed quietly in a grey skirt, grey bodice and white blouse, with a blue and white apron protecting the skirt. She was noticeably pregnant.

The children were fair-haired and neat, like their mother. They stared open-mouthed at Sally and stopped eating.

"This is Emily!" Mrs Stewart introduced the eldest child, a girl of about eight or nine. "And these are Douglas and Jane."

Douglas, an impish-looking child, extended his tiny hand and said "Hellooo!" in a cheeky voice. Mrs Gallagher smiled indulgently at him.

"Sit down and have some breakfast," she invited Sally, "and then we can have a wee chat and I'll tell you what your duties are."

There was already a place set for Sally at the table, much to her gratification. She had heard of households where the hired girl ate at a different table from the family. This was always resented deeply by the girls, who liked to feel they were equal to the families who employed them.

Sally sat down beside Emily and began to eat. The food was similar to what she was used to at home: bread and butter and tea. The children were eating porridge and boiled eggs.

"Why doesn't she get a egg, Mamma?" asked Douglas. "Don't maids eat eggs?"

"I'm sure Sally doesn't want an egg this morning," said

Mrs Stewart quickly. "Hurry up and eat your porridge, Douglas, like a good boy, before it gets cold."

From this exchange Sally understood that she was not entitled to eggs for breakfast. Oh well. She didn't like them anyway. But she felt hurt and less friendly towards Mrs Stewart than she had at first.

Douglas did not give up so easily. "Have you ever seen a hen?" he asked Sally.

"Yes, I have," she answered kindly. She summed him up as a cheeky brat but at least he was talking to her.

"Do they have cows in...Don...the place you came from?"

"Yes they do. We have three cows ourselves. Or we used to."

"What happened to them? Did they run away?"

"No, we sold two of them. We still have one."

"One of our cows ran away. She ran away to Omagh, to the market there. She wanted to get Peggy's Leg."

"I'm not surprised," said Sally. "Peggy's Leg is lovely, isn't it? I love it."

"Me too," said Douglas, grinning at her. His eyes lit up with delight, at the mention of Peggy's Leg, and Sally was reminded strongly of Janey. How Janey loved sweets! When she left this place she was going to bring her home a huge bag of goodies. She would be able to afford them, with all the money she earned.

"Now then," said Mrs Stewart. "I'd better tell you what you will be expected to do here. I don't suppose Willie has given you any instructions?"

"No, ma'am, he hasn't."

Mrs Stewart proceeded to do so. Sally would have to get up early every morning and get the fire going before anyone else got up. She would have to cook the porridge and set the table for breakfast. Then she'd have to go out to the byre and milk the cows, of which there were six. By that time the Stewarts would be up and have breakfasted, and she could come in and take her own morning meal. Afterwards she would make all the beds, sweep the floor and clean the house. Then it would be time to prepare the potatoes for dinner. After dinner there would be various tasks to perform: they churned once a week, there was spinning to be done at all times, bread to be baked every second day, large quantities of sewing and mending. The litany of chores went on. It was all familiar to Sally, well used to the running of a house and farm. The difference was that here she would actually have to work, whereas at home she had usually managed to get someone else to do it.

Even listening to Mrs Stewart, who gathered steam as she progressed through her list and thought of more and more tasks to add to it, made her feel tired. When would she get time to read? Would she ever go for a walk? Would she ever...?

"Please, madam," she said, "when will I be able to see my sister?"

Mrs Stewart looked taken aback. But she had heard about Katie.

"Why, on Sundays, of course."

A gleam of hope.

"Oh, will I be free on Sundays?"

"You will be free to go to church. I suppose that is what you mean? You will meet your sister there, presumably. And you will have one Sunday a month off. We always give our girls a day off every month. Willie insists on that, for some reason. I find it difficult to manage, but we survive."

"I see," said Sally, sadly. Today was Tuesday. That meant

she would not see Katie for five whole days. And she was so curious about her sister's new job!

"You can take your time with things today, since you are still finding your feet." Mrs Stewart wound up her speech on this surprising note. Sally had not expected any respite from the endless tasks which were apparently just begging to be done, according to Mrs Stewart's account. "I thought you might walk to school with Emily, for a start, and get some impression of the surroundings."

"I'd like that," said Sally. "When does she start?"

"It's time to leave already," replied Mrs Stewart. "Emily, get your coat and turf."

Emily obediently left the table, put on her coat, and took a little bag of turf from beside the range. Like many children, she had to take some turf for the schoolhouse fire with her.

"She will show you the way," Mrs Stewart said. "The school is in Brown Knoll, about a mile from here. It's a pleasant walk, you should enjoy it."

Sally did.

The previous night, she had seen little of the countryside she had journeyed through. Now she looked with pleasure at the gently undulating landscape which surrounded the Stewarts' home. Small, picturesque hills rolled away towards the horizon, which was blocked by pale, smoky-blue mountains, rising majestically into the sky. Meandering between the nearby hills was a river, one of the widest, bluest rivers Sally had ever seen.

"It's one of the streams," Emily explained. "In the seven glens there are seven streams."

But she did not know what it, or any of the streams, was called.

They walked along a narrow boreen, bordered by heavy

hedgerows. Occasionally they passed farmhouses, each set in its own neat garden and surrounded by trees. The ground underfoot was covered with leaves of gold and red and yellow, and produced a crunchy rustling sound.

Emily was shy and Sally had to drag conversation out of her. She was eight years old. This was her third year at school. The teacher was Miss Houston and was cross sometimes, but not all the time. She had a friend, yes. The friend was called...

Suddenly, Sally caught sight of a house she thought she recognised.

"Emily," she said, cutting short the description of the friend. "Who lives in that house?"

"That's Campbells'," said Emily. "My friend's name is Jane, just like my little sister's. Her hair is funny, it sticks out. She's eight and a half."

"I have a sister called Jane too," said Sally, absent-mindedly. "Janey, we call her. She's three. She'll be four in December, just before Christmas."

Emily, warming up now, chattered on about Jane, her friend, and about school. She asked Sally a few questions about her life at home, which the latter answered absent-mindedly. So that was Katie's place. It looked shabby enough. Perhaps on the way home she'd catch a glimpse of her?

They reached the school before long. It was a cottage-style building, containing only one classroom. Since it was a cold day the children were allowed to go inside as they arrived and did not have to wait in the yard. Sally brought Emily into the room, and put her little bag of turf at the fireside. The schoolmistress was already at her desk. She did look rather cross, as Emily had said. Sally nodded to her and left quickly.

She trotted quickly along the lane until she came to the Campbells' house. At the garden gate she stopped, and peered through the thick overhanging hedge. The red front door was shut and she could see nothing through the windows of the house: the curtains seemed to be still drawn. A thin wreath of grey smoke snaked up from the chimney, however, indicating that somebody was up inside. Katie?

Sally waited for a few minutes, scrutinising the house. It was quite run-down, especially by comparison with the neat homestead of the Stewarts and of most of the people living in this district, who seemed to have very high standards of home upkeep. This house needed a new thatch, and the whitewash on the walls was flaking off in many places, leaving big grey stains like ink-blots. The doors and windows looked as if they hadn't been painted in donkey's years and the front garden was a tangle of weeds and nettles. There were no dogs, chickens, animals of any kind. The place seemed curiously lifeless.

Sally was gazing, and lost in depressing comparisons between her own lot and Katie's, when she felt a heavy hand on her shoulder. She almost jumped out of her skin with fright.

She turned around.

It was Robert Campbell.

"So?" he said, in a voice which was none too friendly. "What are you staring at?"

"I...I was just wondering...if Katie might come out," Sally stammered.

"Katie has plenty to keep her busy," said Campbell. "You don't be hanging around here, wasting her time. Surely you've got your own job to be doing."

His voice was harsh and cold. Sally could hardly believe

he was the same man who had conversed in such a reasonable and sensible way with her mother the day before.

"Be off with you now, young one. You'll see Katie soon enough."

"Tell her I said hello!" Sally ventured, before she turned and walked sadly away.

8

Come Sunday

Sally had a busy week. Mrs Stewart saw to it that she had few idle moments. There was an endless round of chores to be done in the house and dairy, and at the end of each day Sally flopped into bed, worn out. She wondered if she would last for six months at this hectic pace. Trying to read a few pages, for comfort, before falling to sleep, she doubted it. The work was simply too hard, and there was no respite. Even playing with the children, which she had to do every afternoon between four and five while Mrs Stewart, who often felt tired because of her pregnancy, rested, was a cheerless chore. Sally felt so tired herself! Douglas teased her and pulled her hair and refused to do a single thing she asked. She could not get him to stay quiet, and every time he screeched Mrs Stewart knocked on the ceiling with a stick she kept by her bed for this very purpose. If Douglas were unusually noisy she came down from her rest wearing a grim martyred expression and refused to speak to Sally for hours afterwards. Once she had even said, "I will have to speak to Mr Stewart about this. It just won't do!"

In fact Sally saw very little of William Stewart. All day he was out working on the farm. "Mending fences!" Mrs Stewart said, vaguely. He came in for his dinner at one o'clock and for tea at six or seven. Most evenings, he was out visiting neighbours or going to meetings: he was a president of the local Orange Lodge and had many duties concerned with its organisation. When he stayed at home, he sat by the fire in silence, reading. He had a good collection of books. Sally's heart had leaped with pleasurable anticipation when she had first caught sight of the bookcase in the parlour. But upon examination she realised that most of the books were about agricultural science: they were full of long lists of sheep's diseases and breeds of cattle. The only other books were the Bible and *Old Moore's Almanac*.

The Stewart family didn't see much of their father, either. Nevertheless—or perhaps for that very reason—they all regarded him with profound respect, and deferred to his wishes on every occasion. In his frequent absences, Mrs Stewart interpreted his wishes for everyone's benefit. "Oh, Emily, I don't think your father would like you to wear that green ribbon in your hair! Green is the Parnellites' colour," she would say.

Parnell was the bane of William Stewart's life, according to Mrs Stewart. He had nightmares about him and about Home Rule. Whenever the words were mentioned or hinted at in any way he would become extremely upset. He would either shout and scream, or fall into a deadly sulk from which he might not emerge for hours, or days. It was not good for his health or for anyone else's. The family had to be careful at all times. Even when he wasn't there. The walls had ears. They would somehow indicate to Daddy that some evil name, like Parnell, had been mentioned in their hearing.

Another favourite line of Mrs Stewart's was, "Douglas, your father would want you to tidy your room."

Sometimes it sounded to Sally as if Mrs Stewart had no wishes at all of her own. To hear her speak, you would imagine that she existed only as a substitute for her husband, someone who might just as well disappear into the woodwork if he decided to grace the house with his presence for more than a few hours a week and speak for himself. It seemed that for her own part, she, personally, didn't care one hoot about Home Rule or Charles Stewart Parnell or untidy rooms or misbehaving children. Everything that happened in life was a matter of complete indifference to the real Mrs Stewart. But Sally soon began to suspect that really, Mrs Stewart didn't care what her husband thought about the children or the house or the farm or anything else. She just used his name to fend off any criticism of herself and to add authority to her statements. It was very odd. Sally decided that she would never allow herself to do anything of that kind. If she ever had a husband to defer to, that is. Which seemed unlikely, if she was going to spend half her life living in other people's kitchens, doing their work for them.

She thought of Manus, for a second. It had been nice, talking to him that time in the farmyard. She had talked to him once again, soon after that, when she had been visiting Maura at her house. But not since that: at school they had pointedly ignored one another. The boys and girls kept strictly apart there, and Sally did not have the courage to break the invisible barrier that separated them. Neither, apparently, did Manus. She wished she or he had. It would have been great to get to know him: she knew they could have been good friends. But it seemed that that could not happen now. He was still at school, still living at home, while she was far away, working for her living. A hired girl. He probably wouldn't want to know a hired girl anyway. She tried not to think of him, most of the time. And most of the time she didn't.

There was so much else to think of. She had so many immediate problems. She had always hated housework, and now she had to do it all day long. She tried to get away with completing her tasks as easily as possible, cutting corners whenever she could. If Mrs Stewart noticed, which she did only now and then, because she was so tired that she hadn't the energy to check everything, she got angry and shouted. Sally wanted to shout back, but she couldn't. She just had to stand there and listen, in silence, while she was told off in no uncertain terms. It was maddening.

She didn't get on well with the children, either, at first. Jane was just a baby, and Sally had no interest in her. Douglas was as bold as brass and a constant thorn in her side. She had to admit that Emily was a friendly and pleasant little girl, but she didn't want to make friends with her: she was one of the Stewarts, after all. The boss's daughter. Why should she, Sally, bother getting to know her?

The worst problem of all was homesickness. She missed her mother much more than she would have imagined possible: she had never spent all that much time with her mother when she was at home. But now she realised how much she loved her. She missed her funny old grandmother, whom she had always considered an embarrassment and a nuisance. And when she thought of Janey she felt like crying. She was homesick for the house and valley almost as much as for her family. She dreamed of them, sometimes, although not most of the time. The fact was that a lot of her dreams were about the housework she had to do during the day: they were nightmares, in which she had to milk hundreds of cows or wash mountains of dirty delph. But occasionally she did dream of home, of the sights and sounds of the valley. The farmhouse. The trees in the yard. The waves lapping against the shore. The sound of the sea was one of the things she found it hardest to do without. And the sound of people talking her own language. She had no problem speaking English: she had always been good at it and had read so much that she had a better vocabulary than most native English speakers. But she was missing the sound of Irish now. Like the sound of the sea, it had been in her ears since the moment she was born. It is hard to get used to a new set of sounds.

The only consolation was that Katie was in the neighbourhood. Just knowing that made everything bearable. She wished she could see her more often than once a week. But it was better than nothing. Much better. Whenever she felt that she really had had as much as she could take, she thought of Sunday, when she and Katie would meet. If she could hold out till Sunday, she would be all right.

9

A Long Sermon

Sunday came at last, a bright and sunny day. Sally jumped out of bed with more eagerness than she had been able to muster on any other morning and dressed in her best frock and long black stockings. Both dress and stockings had been hanging on a hook behind the door waiting for this occasion. She ran downstairs two steps at a time and prepared breakfast for the Stewarts, who would eat before going to their own church or "kirk" as they called it. Then she took a bowl of porridge and a cup of milk for herself, her usual breakfast. But when Mrs Stewart came down, looking very elegant, in spite of her fat tummy, in a black silk dress with a white collar, she insisted that Sally eat a fried egg and rasher as well, since it was Sunday. Sally was so anxious to be off that she did not enjoy the meal as much as she should have but the news that she would get a special Sunday breakfast made her heart glow warmly inside her. Mrs Stewart was funny: changeable, was the best way to describe her. Sometimes Sally thought she could get to like her. But then she would suddenly change, become cross and shout at her. She never knew where she was with Mrs Stewart. She was quite unpredictable.

Finally breakfast was over and Sally was allowed to go, at about eight o'clock. Mass was at nine, and the church was three miles away in the village of Ballygowl, so she had to walk briskly in order to get there in time. There were other walkers on the little road and a few donkeys and carts. Sally had hoped that she might see Katie and be able to go part of the way with her, but there was no sign of her sister.

She arrived in Ballygowl at five minutes to nine. The tiny Catholic church was at the far end of the town, at the opposite end from the Presbyterian chapel, which looked down over the main street from a high windy hill. Sally walked quickly along the street, hardly having time to get a good look at the shops and houses that lined the way. She reached the church on the stroke of nine and pushed her way through the throng of men and boys at the door. Inside, the place was packed, women sitting at one side and men at the other. There were some empty places in a pew about three rows up, so she slid into one of them. From this vantage point she could see most but not all of the church. She immediately scanned all the seats on the women's side, searching for Katie, but the latter was not to be seen. Could she be on the men's side? No. Or behind? Sally peered over her shoulder, trying to see, but she couldn't examine the pews behind properly. Katie must be in one of them, or standing right at the back.

She thought Mass would never end. The priest was one of the long-winded types who liked to preach until everyone was dropping dead from exhaustion. His sermon lasted for at least half an hour. It seemed ten times longer to Sally, even though the subject matter was quite interesting: he spoke about politics, which had not much to do with the gospel of the day. But he managed to forge some kind of unlikely link between the two topics. A local election was coming off in the area, it seemed. He wanted his parishioners to vote for the Home Rule candidate. Parnell, he said, was the saviour of Ireland. A good Protestant with his heart in the right place. He had the breeding, the intelligence, and the education to know how to handle the English. He was clever enough to be able to handle the trickiest man ever known in political history, the English prime minister, William Gladstone. All who had a vote should give their support to Parnell. Everyone who did not have a vote should encourage those who had to give their vote to Parnell. And so on and so forth.

Will you for God's sake stop, thought Sally. I've got more important matters than Parnell to attend to. I don't have a vote. Most of the people in this church don't have a vote for one reason or another. Most of them haven't enough land to be allowed to vote. Or else they're women and they can't vote at all, no matter how rich they are. Or they're too young. Sally was all three. Too young, too poor and a woman. There was no way she would ever be able to support Parnell or anyone else. There was no way she would be able to do anything about getting Home Rule for Ireland or not getting it. Why should she have to listen to this boring old man going on and on about it?

Eventually he gave up, grabbed a glass of water from a considerate or terrified altar boy, and returned to the business of getting through Mass. Sally breathed a sigh of relief. And indeed the priest, realising that he had kept the congregation rather longer than was permissible, raced through the rest of the ceremony, with the result that it was all over about five minutes after the end of the sermon. Great, thought Sally, getting out of her pew as fast as she could and dashing to the door.

She waited.

The irreligious men left first. They walked from the church door where they had been leaning, talking and smoking, to the wall at the other side of the road, and leaned against that and talked and smoked there instead. Katie was not, of course, among them, being neither irreligious nor a man.

Next came the religious men. They walked silently and sedately out, nodded politely to their acquaintances, saying "Grand morning!" and moved along the road, homeward.

They were followed by the boys. The boys tumbled out of the door, thumping one another in the ribs, giving each other unfriendly and friendly kicks, pulling off caps, pinching ears. They didn't talk much but they grinned and laughed and let out yells. "Hey! Paddy! Take that!" "What hit ye, Mickey? Ha ha!"

Finally the women and girls emerged, huddling together in little groups. Their low voices preceded them like a softly threatening breeze. Pwsh pwsh, pwsh pwsh! Whispers floated in the air around them, excluding everyone from the gossiping flocks.

Katie was not with them.

Sally waited...and waited. Finally she went back into the church and had a look. Nobody there.

She stood outside the door again and waited.

After a while the priest came out, wearing his three-cornered biretta. He nodded to Sally, didn't speak, and she watched him swinging down the road in his long black skirts. Swish, went the skirts, swish out of my way, everybody: I'm the priest. Swish swish!

Then a man wearing a long black coat, in imitation of the priest's, came out. He had a big hump on his back and a nose like an eagle's beak. He was carrying a huge iron key. With the key he locked the door of the chapel. He stared at

Sally, said "Humph!" and humped away down the road.

Sally looked disconsolately at the yew trees and laurel bushes that grew by the walls of the church. It was, she guessed, unlikely that Katie was hiding in them, playing a mean practical joke.

She had to accept the truth. Katie was not here.

Her eyes filled with tears.

She had looked forward to this meeting all week. It was the one thing that had kept her going. She had not even realised how important it was, until now. Katie. Her very last link with home, with her family. The only person in this whole great bleak place that knew her and loved her.

And she wasn't here.

Life didn't seem worth living.

She might as well give up now. She might as well be dead.

Weeping copiously, she began to walk slowly back towards the Stewarts' farm.

10

A Visit to Campbells'

As she walked along the country road, Sally's tears gradually dried up. She looked at the calm green fields and at the ditches where blackberries still dangled on their hooking brambles, and at the cows waddling through the grass. And she began to feel calmer herself. Perhaps there was some perfectly natural explanation for Katie's absence. Perhaps she wasn't feeling well enough to take the long walk, or maybe some crisis had occurred in the house. The old woman might be ill. Old women often were.

Sally decided that she would not go straight home. Instead she would call on the Campbells and find out what the matter was. There was no point in worrying about them all day. And in this way she would see Katie and get a chance to exchange a few words with her.

Once this decision was made, Sally felt very much better. The spring returned to her step and she walked briskly along, so that in quite a short time she was at the Campbells' gate. Her heart was in her boots as she pushed it open and found herself in the overgrown garden. The path to the door was overhung with heavy branches, which she had to push out of the way as she approached it. Just as she reached the shabby old door, a dog began to bark very sharply. Sally almost jumped out of her skin. She knocked hard on the door. The dog came running around the side of the house, snarling viciously. He raced up and began to snap at her heels. Sally tried not to scream. She had been taught—by her father—that dogs smell fear, and attack anyone who shows it. Sally knocked for the second time at the door. Out of the corner of her eye she noticed a grimy curtain being pulled back from one of the grimy windows. The next minute the door was pulled open. She jumped inside with great speed, and leaned back against the closed door in relief.

Sally was shaking so much that she could take no notice of anything for at least five minutes. She lay against the door, trembling. Her stomach felt nauseated and her head dizzy. She thought she was probably about to faint.

After a few minutes, however, she felt a little better. She looked up and saw Katie smiling at her. Katie was holding her hand. Just behind Katie, staring over her shoulder, was the oddest-looking old woman Sally had ever seen.

Old Mrs Campbell.

The first thing you noticed about her was her hair. She was wearing a little white lace cap, the kind that all married women or older women wore. But her hair was not tucked up under it, out of harm's way, as it should have been. Instead it streamed down like a young girl's, curling all over her shoulders. A mixture of iron grey and snow white. Amazing!

And then you noticed her nose, which was long and beaky and bony, the kind of nose lots of old people had, only bigger than most.

Unlike most old women, however, she did not have a pale face. Her cheeks were as rosy as apples. And her eyes were not watery and vapid. They were a brilliant forget-me-not blue. They twinkled like stars in her funny, rosy face. Twinkled mischievously.

Her clothes were odd enough too, although not half as odd as her face. She wore a long black dress. Over it was an apron, striped in brilliant green and white and purple, and over her shoulders a plaid shawl, in red and black and blue. Quite a colour sensation, she created, in the dark and gloomy kitchen.

Katie and Sally gazed at one another, clasping each other's hands and smiling. They could not think of a word to say.

"Who are you?" asked the old lady, old Mrs Campbell, in her croaky old lady voice. "Don't tell me, let me guess. You're Katie's sister. So the next question is, what are you doing here?"

"I came...I came to see Katie!" mumbled Sally. "She wasn't at Mass. I thought she'd be at Mass, but...but...but..."

"Humph! Mass! I never go to church myself; it bores me to tears. Why should your sister waste her time with it when I don't? Why do you waste your time with it yourself?"

"Well...I..."

But Sally could come up with no answer to that.

"What did the papist puppet tell you anyway? Don't tell me; don't tell me. Let me guess. I bet he told you to vote for ould Parnell, didn't he? Isn't that what he told ye? Vote for ould Parnell. Ha? Didn't he?"

"Yes," said Sally.

"Always the same. Week in week out. Vote for Parnell. They'll change their tune. Mark my words: they'll be changing their tune soon enough. I've seen it in the tea-leaves. A big change is on the way and Parnell will tumble from his pedestal into the dust where he belongs. Ashes to ashes and dust to dust. He's flesh and blood, the same Parnell, flesh and blood like all of us. Like me and like you. Like me and like you."

Sally and Katie exchanged a glance, but did not say anything.

"So ye wondered why your sister was not at chapel? No maid of mine will waste her time at chapel listening to nonsense from papish puppets, no indeed. Time is too valuable. Life is too short for that sort of carry-on when there's lots of work to be done. Will ye have a cup of tea?"

"Thank you," said Sally, astonished. "I will."

"Give your sister a cup of tea, girsha," said Mrs Campbell. Katie got some cups from a dresser and poured out tea.

They sat down by the fire.

"So how are they treatin' you up at William Stewart's?" asked the old woman, with a toothy laugh.

"The best," said Sally. "They're treating me the best."

"Och aye, I bet they are," said Mrs Campbell. "I bet they are, the same Stewarts. They'll get their penny's worth out of ye, I can tell ye that. That Maggie one...isn't that her name?"

"Aye," said Sally. "Mrs Stewart. Maggie, I think, she is."

"She's a right wee skutter, that one. I mind her as a wean around here, cheeky wee brat she was, full of back answers. I mind one time she were down here helping—supposed to be helping—with the haymaking. 'Will ye bring this can of tea down to the men in the field?' I asked her. 'I'm not your servant,' she said, as cheeky as pie. Och aye..." She gave way to a burst of laughter, which ended in a spluttering cough. Katie had to pat her on the back about fifty times to get the coughing to stop.

By then the tea was finished and Katie and Sally left the kitchen.

11

Divorce!

"**S**he's weird," said Sally, as soon as they got out on the road. "Isn't she?"

Katie looked over her shoulder. She leaned against Sally's face and whispered, "She's more than that. She's a witch."

"Really?" Sally's eyes opened wide, in an attempt to convey astonishment. But she was not all that surprised. She had assumed old Mrs Campbell was a witch the minute she set eyes upon her. Anyone could tell. From her long grey hair. And her rosy-apple cheeks. And her strange, piercing eyes. Everything about her appearance proclaimed loudly, "I am the witch of all your dreams and nightmares!"

"Yes." Katie drew away from Sally and spoke at a normal pitch. Her voice still shook like a poplar leaf, however. "She's a real old witch. She boils herbs and things in a black pot and makes medicines out of them. And she buries bits of meat in William Stewart's fields. When the meat rots the Stewarts will lose the good of the fields. That's what she thinks, anyhow. She hates the Stewarts."

"Does she?" asked Sally, genuinely surprised this time. "I thought they were friends."

"William and Robert are friends. They're friends, all right. But she hates them. She hates them partly for that reason. She thinks William is a bad influence on Robert, keeping him out late at meetings and things, and drinking with him. And she hates Maggie Stewart. You've heard her going on about her. She hopes she has bad luck. I'd be worried, if I were Maggie Stewart, and expecting the baby and all."

"She's had three children already. I don't suppose there's such a danger with this one."

"Well. There will be if Old Mother Campbell can help it. I'd stay out of her way, if I were Maggie Stewart. She'll put the eye on her."

"Has she the evil eye?"

"More than one, if you ask me. Both her eyes are as evil as they come. You don't want to get on the wrong side of her, believe me."

"What else has she done?"

"Isn't that enough? She's always doing things. She's busy all day long, collecting stuff out in the ditches and making concoctions, and making plans. She's always planning what she's going to do next, who she's going to attack."

"It must be frightening for you. It must be awful, oh, poor Katie."

Sally put her arms around her sister and gave her a big hug.

"It is awful. But I'm used to her by now, almost. And she seems to like me, so far."

"Have you got a lot of work to do? Is it hard?"

"Not really, not as much as I used to do at home. Robert does everything on the farm. I've just got to do the house and make sure the dinner is ready when he comes in. But usually she does the dinner herself. She's good at that, I must say. She can cook..."

"I'd hate to have to eat the stuff she cooks."

"It's the only thing there is to eat. And it's all right. It's nice, in fact. Stews with rabbits and pheasant, roast chicken. They've very good bacon, too. They're well off, even though the place looks so horrible."

Sally reached into the hedgerow and pulled some blackberries from a bramble which was hidden deep in the dying foliage. She handed half of them to her sister and they chewed the rather withered berries in silence.

"Why does the place look such a mess, if they are well off?"

"It's because she can't be bothered with how it looks, or with doing anything about it. She's so busy, all the time, with her medicines and her spells and her evil wicked plans and everything. She's working all day long at those things. You can't imagine how busy she is. There is simply not a minute to spare for housework."

Sally paused and thought of Mrs Stewart, buzzing around in her neat, lovely home. She thought of Mrs Stewart's large, blue, but sad eyes.

"So it's not so bad there, then?"

"Not at the moment. No, it's not so bad. I mean it's very strange and it's lonely, because there's nobody to talk to most of the time except her. And Robert in the evenings."

"Listen, Katie," she said. "If anything happens. You know. If anything goes wrong there, ever, with him or her, promise you'll tell me. Tell me before it happens. If there are any warnings."

"I'm telling you now. Odd things happen every day. She's sitting there making spells. He's sitting there saying absolutely nothing, staring at me. What am I supposed to do about it?"

Sally was silent. The fact was, there was nothing they could do about it. They were stuck.

"Well, he seemed OK to me. Trustworthy, I thought."

"Yes, he probably is. I'm not worried about him. She's not what you'd call trustworthy, though, is she? I mean, you wouldn't trust her as far as you could throw her, would you?"

They had come some distance along the road by now, and Sally decided that, reluctant as she was to leave Katie, she would have to go home. So they said goodbye and promised to meet again the following Sunday. Katie thought she might be able to get away some time during the week. Mrs Campbell was not the sort who would mind, or even notice, if she walked over to Stewarts' for a few hours some afternoon. With the prospect of an early meeting, they parted not too unhappily.

Some weeks passed.

Sally became more accustomed to her work and to her employers. She was never sure of where she stood with Mrs Stewart. But in general she got on reasonably well with her and was beginning to like her: she could see that Mrs Stewart was not feeling very well a lot of the time, and that that was probably what made her so moody. She noticed that Emily, with whom she was becoming very friendly, was also wary of her mother.

Katie did not manage to visit Sally on weekdays; Mrs Campbell always needed her to help with some job, just at the wrong moment. But after the first Sunday she was allowed to go to Mass, and met her sister there. They had a long, good walk together afterwards, often finishing up with a cup of tea and a chat with old Mrs Campbell. Sally enjoyed talking to the old woman. She was certainly very odd but she was lively and interesting. You never knew what she would say next.

One Sunday she stayed longer than she should have at the Campbell cottage. Mrs Campbell had been telling them stories about her youth at the beginning of the century. It was so fascinating that Sally lost track of the time. When she got back to the Stewarts, they were preparing to sit down to their midday dinner. "Oh dear," thought Sally, "I'm for it now." But Mrs Stewart just smiled at her and said "Hello, dear," and Mr Stewart winked. So they were both in a good mood, apparently. Sally joined them at the table and they began to eat in silence. Corned beef, cabbage and potatoes. What they always had on Sundays. On weekdays they had bacon and cabbage, or sometimes just potatoes and butter.

As usual, Douglas pushed his food around his plate, broke it up into tiny pieces, slipped bits of meat and potato on to the floor when he thought it was safe to do so, and generally tried to get away with not eating a single bite. Emily and Jane observed him and smirked knowingly at one another, waiting for their father to notice what was going on and shout at Douglas. Usually he noticed after about five minutes, and then some kind of entertainment was guaranteed to relieve the boredom of the family meal. Unfortunately, today, Mr Stewart was lost in thought. While he kept silence, nobody else spoke either.

"What was that Annie Dunbar was saying to you outside the chapel this morning?" Finally, he looked up from his cabbage and directed this question at his wife.

"Och, some nonsense about that Parnell fellow," said Mrs Stewart, shrugging her shoulders nervously. "She was saying that he's soon going to be in trouble again, even though he did well out of that *Times* business."

"Surely," said William Stewart, smiling. "We all know that. He'll be caught this time, and no mistake. And there'll be no more talk about Home Rule for another hundred years."

"Never, I hope," said Mrs Stewart, piously.

"Did they mention Parnell at the RC church?"

At first Sally didn't realise that she was being addressed. William Stewart had hardly ever spoken to her, since he brought her here. He had to repeat his question.

"Yes," she said. "The priest said something about him. I didn't pay much attention, I'm afraid. Actually, he says something about Parnell more or less every Sunday. He seems to like him."

Mr Stewart laughed. "He won't like him for much longer. The papists will never stand for this divorce business. The priests put Parnell in and now they'll bring him down. If there's one thing they can't stand it's women."

"Please, Willie, not in front of the children," said Mrs Stewart.

"What's divorce, Papa?" asked Emily, looking up from her plate in puzzlement.

"William!" warned Mrs Stewart.

"The girl might as well know, Maggie," he retorted. "They all might as well know, because they'll be hearing about it soon enough. With this Parnell affair, I mean. There'll be nothing but divorce in the papers and on people's tongues over the next couple of months, mark my words."

He turned to Emily, who was sitting open-mouthed.

"Divorce is when two married people decide to stop being married to one another," he said. "That's all it means."

"But why would they do that?" asked Emily.

"Well, they might not get on with one another any more. That might be the reason."

"And does Parnell not get on with his wife any more?"

"No. He hasn't got a wife. But he wants to marry a woman who is already married to another man."

"He can't do that," said Emily, with an air of finality.

"He can if her husband divorces her," said Mr Stewart.

"And will he do that?"

"I would if I were him," said Mr Stewart.

Jane started to howl.

"What's the matter?" asked Sally, patting her on the head. "Did you swallow something the wrong way?"

Jane continued to scream at the top of her lungs.

Mrs Stewart looked at her husband and shook her head.

"What is it, Jane?" she asked. "Tell me what's wrong."

"Are...are...are you and Papa going to get divorced?" she sobbed out.

Mrs Stewart glared at Mr Stewart.

"Now see what you've done!" she said. She turned to Jane and began to reassure her. Mr Stewart got up, pushed his chair against the table and walked out of the kitchen, slamming the door. Douglas dropped the last piece of meat from his plate on to the floor, smiled sweetly at his mother and said, "Finished!"

For once, nobody bothered to contradict him. Because, at that moment, Mrs Stewart suddenly turned pale and clutched her stomach.

"It's starting," she said to Sally.

12

A New Baby

"**S**tarting" meant starting to have the baby. Sally knew that, the minute Mrs Stewart spoke. Anyone would have known what she meant. But Sally pretended not to understand. Even to herself, she pretended that. She had heard her own mother saying similar words, the time her little sister was born, just four years ago. What it had meant for Sally was that she was whisked off to a neighbour's, where she stayed for a few days, having the time of her life. When she came home again, Janey was wrapped up in a white blanket, tucked in beside Mother in bed. Mother stayed in bed for another couple of weeks and Dad stayed in the house as much as possible, looking after her and the rest of the family. It had been, as far as Sally was concerned, a festive fortnight. Like a great holiday.

But now, she guessed, she would be expected to help Mrs Stewart. And she didn't want to do that. She didn't want to have any involvement with the whole mysterious business of having a baby. She didn't want to know about it.

"I'm starting!" Mrs Stewart repeated, less anxiously and with more impatience. "Go and get Mr Stewart, please."

Sally ran out of the house into the farmyard. Mr Stewart was deftly saddling his horse, preparing to go on a good long gallop.

"Mr Stewart, Mr Stewart!" she shouted at him from across the yard. "Mrs Stewart is starting!"

Holding the stirrup strap in his hand, he turned and looked at her. His face was stony.

For a moment he was speechless.

He continued to saddle the mare. He did not say a word until he had mounted her.

"Tell her," he said, "that I'm getting the handywoman."

And with that he kicked the mare's flanks and left the yard at a smart canter. Sally watched him as he rode down the road, and then, opening a gate and entering a long field, galloped speedily off.

Slowly she went back to the kitchen and told Mrs Stewart what he had said.

"I'm going up to bed," she said with a sigh. "You come up and help me undress. Emily can look after the children for the minute."

Emily ran over to her mother and asked anxiously, "Are you all right, Mother?"

"I'll be worse before I'm better," said Mrs Stewart, smiling wanly at her elder daughter. Emily's eyes filled with tears. Mrs Stewart held her close and said: "Don't worry, my dear. I'm going to be fine. You mind Douglas and Jane and make sure they don't come to any harm while Sally is helping me. Papa will be home in no time at all."

Mrs Stewart's big eyes softened as she spoke to Emily, and for a while she looked happy. She really did love her children, Sally thought, feeling sorry for her.

Sally patted Emily on the head. Then she followed Mrs Stewart up to her bedroom. She helped her take off her flowing grey frock, and her lace petticoats, and put on a large white nightgown. Mrs Stewart climbed into bed and propped herself up against the bolster. Sally folded her clothes and put them on a chair.

"Open that chest, Sally," said Mrs Stewart then, "and take out three of the big towels and the baby's dress."

Sally looked around the simply furnished room. Against the wall under the window was a large wooden chest, one of the few large objects, apart from the bed, in the room. She opened it. A spicy smell of mothballs emerged. The chest was filled with snow-white linen: sheets and underwear and towels and infants' clothing, all sewed neatly by Mrs Stewart herself. She took out three white towels and a tiny white dress, edged with exquisite broderie anglaise, and brought them over to Mrs Stewart. She examined them.

"That's right," she nodded approvingly. "Now put them on top of the chest until we need them."

Sally did so. She glanced out the window to see if there was any sign of Mr Stewart, but there wasn't. She could see the children, playing Pussy Four Corners in the yard. Their small tinny voices rose on the still cold air and fell like the notes of a distant piano into the bedroom. As Sally listened to the haunting sound, she was moved. Children. How lovely they were, even the boldest! Even Douglas, when you observed him happily playing, listened to his little high-pitched voice singing, was charming. And innocent. Sally's eyes filled with tears and her heart felt hot and jumpy. Her own childhood was slipping away from her. She could almost feel it, sliding through her fingers. That she was reluctant to let it go did not matter. That would not slow up the process in the slightest. It was not fair; it was not fair! She was only thirteen, just a few years older than Emily, out there playing in the yard. She did not feel ready to grow up.

"Oh!" said Mrs Stewart suddenly, clutching her high stomach. "Ouch!"

"Can I do something for you?" Sally ran to the bedside. She spoke in a kind voice. "Would you like a cup of tea? Some water?"

Mrs Stewart's face was contorted slightly with pain. She did not speak for a minute. Then she smiled and said, "A cup of tea would be nice, just now. Later I won't be able to have any."

Sally ran downstairs, relieved to escape for a few minutes from the room.

While she was wetting the tea, the children came rushing into the kitchen, shouting, "Annie Borland's coming over the road; Annie Borland's coming over the road!"

Sally heaved a sigh of relief, and fetched a second cup from the dresser.

Annie Borland was a stout woman of about forty-five. She had small intelligent blue eyes and a comical nose. Her hair curled out from under her lace cap, black as bogwater.

Sally had met women like Annie before. "Handywomen," they were known as. That is to say, they were a kind of unofficial nurses. There were very few doctors around in the countryside at this time, and most people couldn't afford to use them anyway. Unless they were at death's door, they preferred to call on someone like Annie Borland. These handywomen officiated at all births. Another thing they did was lay out the dead. So they were present at the beginning and end of human life. This seemed to give them an insight into people's minds that few others possessed.

You could tell at a glance, anyway, that Annie Borland was an exceptional person. She radiated competence and good humour. And wisdom. She was also completely sure of herself, in the most natural and unobtrusive way.

"You're the hired girl, then?" Annie said, as soon as she walked in the door. Even though her face was not what you could call attractive, she had a very sweet smile. It cheered Sally up to see it. "Sally, they tell me your name is? Aren't you the lovely-looking lassie!"

This was just what Sally liked to hear. She beamed and offered Annie a cup of tea, which was accepted.

"And how's the patient? When did she start?"

Sally told her.

"Och, she's got plenty of time. I'll take my sup of tea while I have the chance! Sure I might as well. And that'll give us a chance to get acquainted. Now you take a wee cup of tea yourself like a good girl and tell me all about yourself. I've heard a lot of great things about you, but nothing about who you are or what you are. Do you know what I mean? What part of Donegal do you come from?"

Sally poured some tea for herself and sat down. She had not had a real chat with anyone since she left home. Oddly, neither Mr nor Mrs Stewart had expressed much interest in her background. They never asked her about her home or her family, or about anything that had happened to her in the long years she had lived away from them. It was as if they didn't care to know that she had a life outside of the four walls of their house. As far as they were concerned, she existed only in relation to themselves and their needs.

It was, indeed, so long since Sally had had an ordinary chat with a grown-up that she hardly knew where to start. But Annie knew the right questions to ask, and in a surprisingly short time she had got most of the relevant information out of Sally. By then her tea was finished. She stood up with a very quick light movement, for such a strongly built woman, and she said briskly, "Now I'll go up to her ladyship. You stay here and look after the house. If I need help I'll give you a shout."

Sally looked taken aback. So she was not going to see the whole thing, after all.

Annie Borland understood her look.

"You don't want to be bothered with Mrs Stewart, now. She'll want to be left in peace. And I'll tell you something for nothing. The most amazing thing in the world, and the best, is childbirth. But it's much more wonderful when you're doing it yourself than when you're watching someone else doing it. You keep the fun for yourself, to enjoy in your own time. Which won't be for a good many years yet."

"All right," said Sally. She felt a burden slipping off her shoulders, like a cloak that is too heavy but you don't realise it until it's gone. She went out to the yard and hunted for the children, who at this stage were scattered all over the farm.

Annie Borland came down again a few times, during the next few hours, and had a cup of tea with Sally. Then, at about six o'clock, she went up to the bedroom and did not come down again. Mrs Stewart, who had been quiet and calm, became more vocal. They could hear occasional cries in the kitchen. The children, especially Emily, were frightened. Sally calmed them as best she could, although she felt rather frightened herself. She boiled them eggs, which they regarded as a treat, for supper, and toasted some bread in front of the fire. But at intervals throughout the meal the noises from upstairs stopped the childish conversation, and caused Emily and Jane to stare at Sally with wide, terrified eyes. It was a relief when supper was over. Sally asked the children to get ready for bed, and promised to tell them a long, long story. They were so subdued that for once they obeyed without a murmur, and in no time at all were gathered around the fireside, listening to Sally. She told them the longest and best fairy-tale she knew, the story she had last heard at her own father's wake, about the boy who killed a fearful dragon and, after many adventures, married a princess. Sally recounted the tale as fully and as vividly as was in her powers. They were considerable, and the little audience was so wrapped up in the story that they no longer even remembered what was happening upstairs.

By the time the hero and the princess were getting married at a wedding feast that lasted seven days and seven nights, Douglas was lying in Sally's arms, almost asleep, and the girls were rubbing their eyes.

"Now, to bed, all of you," said Sally, kindly. "I'll carry up this fellow!"

She had hardly set foot on the stair when a loud scream pierced her ears. She jumped out of her skin. But the girls were looking at each other with serious quiet expressions on their faces.

"That's the new baby!" Emily said, calmly.

And Sally realised that that is exactly what it was.

She put Douglas into his bed and came back to the girls.

"You might as well stay here," she said, "so you can see your new brother. Or sister."

She looked around the kitchen. Where was Mr Stewart? In the excitement of the afternoon, she had forgotten what had happened earlier, and had carried on as if he were around the place somewhere. But now she suddenly realised that he had not been at home in five or six hours.

Annie Borland appeared at the top of the stairs and shouted down, "Sally! Come up here and give me a hand!"

Sally ran up the stairs, two steps at a time.

The bedroom was no longer the cool, neat place it had been earlier in the day. There were heaps of sheets and towels on the floor. Two or three buckets sat near the bed, which was itself a jumble of quilts and blankets. Against the bolster Mrs Stewart lay. Her eyes were half-open. Her fair hair was matted and soaked in perspiration, plastered against her head. Her normally narrow oval-shaped face was puffed out and her normally warm complexion was a dull yellow colour.

Annie was carrying a small white bundle.

"It's a wee girl," she said. "Another wee girl."

"Is she all right?" asked Sally, not daring to look.

"She's perfect. The baby is perfect. But she's given her mother a hard time, and no mistake. Och, she's old for it."

"Old?"

Sally had never thought much about Mrs Stewart's age. But she looked young enough to her.

"She's forty if she's a day. It's never easy once you pass the forty. It isn't easy anymore, after that."

She walked up and down, nursing the baby to her large bosom.

"I'll have to let her sleep for a few hours. Listen, girl, will you get a big tub of water ready downstairs, to wash these dirty sheets in? The baby's washed already."

"The girls would like to see the baby," Sally said.

"Och aye, I'll bring her down to them right now. No sign of that father of theirs yet, is there?"

"No."

"He'll be back soon, I don't doubt. The men are all the same. As soon as there's a spot of trouble, they're away."

Not until about eleven o'clock that night did William Stewart return. Emily and Jane, delighted with their new baby sister, were in bed by then and soundly asleep. Sally and Annie Borland were sitting in Mrs Stewart's bedroom. Sally was holding the baby and Annie Borland was tending to Mrs Stewart. By now she was tossing and turning on her bed, gripped by a high fever.

13

Send for the Doctor

William Stewart came home at about midnight. Sally was still up, sitting by the kitchen fire. The children were asleep and Annie Borland was asleep too, sunk in a big wooden chair by the side of Mrs Stewart's bed.

Sally started when she heard the latch lifted, and looked up, wide-eyed, at Mr Stewart. His eyes were bleary and his footsteps unsteady.

"Oh!" exclaimed Sally. "You're home."

"East west; home is best," he said, chuckling in a not very pleasant way. "Tell me all. I'm prepared for anything."

"You have a new daughter," said Sally in a steady voice. She was beginning to feel irritated. "She is asleep upstairs, in the cradle. Mrs Stewart had a difficult delivery and is not well."

"Another girl! Wonderful!"

Now Sally felt really annoyed.

"Annie Borland is still upstairs looking after your wife. If it wasn't for her...I don't know what would have happened."

Mr Stewart was at the dresser, fumbling around among

the cups. He extracted a bottle of whiskey from a hidden corner and poured a generous measure into a teacup.

"Here's to the new child!" he said, swaying a little. "Do join in the celebrations...what's your name?"

"No, thank you," said Sally. She stood up and walked to the door. As she passed him, he tried to grab her but she skipped quickly out of range and he was too drunk to be able to catch her. "Goodnight, Mr Stewart. I'm going to bed."

Next morning, Sally got up early. When she came into the kitchen, she saw William Stewart slumped across the table, fast asleep. The empty whiskey bottle was on the floor beside him and he was snoring.

Sally took away the bottle and put it behind the dresser, before calling down the children. They were all sitting around in their nightclothes, nervously waiting for their porridge, when Annie Borland came heavily downstairs.

"How is she?" asked Sally, with some apprehension, since Annie's expression made it clear that all was not well.

"Not so well," said Annie. "Very poorly."

She sighed deeply, and went over to the dresser.

"The baby will have to go on a bottle. She's not going to be able to feed her herself: she hasn't got the strength. Here she's got a whole set of nice glass bottles with them rubber teats ready. She's a wonderful woman, the same Maggie! She knew something like this might happen. Here, you, scald one of them bottles for me and boil about a cup of milk with three spoons of sugar in it for the child. I'll make a sup of tea for herself."

Sally had sometimes prepared bottles for her sister Janey when the latter was a baby, so she knew how to go about it. Emily came and organised the porridge for her brother and sister, and Annie sat down and drank a cup of tea. A tense hush, broken only by the heavy breathing of William Stewart, filled the room. Everyone was waiting for something to happen.

At last it did. He woke up.

He was one of those people who wake up very rapidly. One moment he was dead to the world, the next he was sitting up, wide awake, staring at everyone with bright, inquisitive eyes. Douglas had exactly the same habit, Sally had noticed.

"Good morning," he said cheerfully, as if it were the most natural thing in the world to have gone to bed on the kitchen table. "And how is the patient today?"

"If you've any sense," said Annie Borland, "you'll get the doctor as soon as you've drunk a sup of tay."

With an alarmed expression on his unshaven face, William Stewart bounded up the stairs.

He returned a few moments later, the baby in his arms.

"The child is crying!" he said, stroking the tiny thing on the head. "She must be hungry."

"I'm making a bottle of milk for her," said Sally.

"A bottle is not what she needs," he said crossly.

"It's what she'll have to be satisfied with, then," said Annie Borland firmly. "Unless you can find someone to nurse her for you."

"I'd prefer that," he said. "You must know of somebody. There's always someone with a baby around here. Tell me, who can I get?"

"Och, I'll think about it," said Annie, wearily. "This child will manage fine on a bottle for a day or two, she's a strong wee one. It's your wife you should be worrying about, not her."

"I'm on my way to fetch Kane now. Don't nag, woman!"

he said.

"Won't you have breakfast?" asked Sally.

"No," he said shortly, and left.

Sally helped the children to dress, and sent Emily off to school. Annie went back to the sickroom, taking the baby with her. Sally was busily engaged for the next few hours, carrying out her own and Mrs Stewart's jobs around the house and in the farmyard. Jane tried to help and was able to do a few things, like feeding the chickens. Douglas, whose confident cheekiness was quickly restored once a semblance of normality returned to the household, hindered all these activities to the best of his abilities. When Sally asked him to carry a bucket for her to the cowhouse, he pretended not to be able to walk, and spent the next hour or so creeping around the floor like a baby, saying, "Oh dear, my legs won't work, my legs won't work." Eventually Sally carried the bucket herself, whereupon Douglas immediately regained the use of his short, plump legs, and used them to chase the chickens all over the garden.

She was so busy that the time flew by. Before she knew it, it was mid-morning. She went up to Annie to see how Mrs Stewart was. The curtains had been drawn and the sickroom was shadowy. In the dimness the bedstead loomed larger than life; its brass rails and snowy quilt gleamed with an eerie moonshine glow. Mrs Stewart's laboured breathing swelled on the otherwise dead-still, sourish air.

At first, Sally could not see Annie and a cold fear grabbed her heart: had the old woman abandoned her, and left her, alone, with...this? But when her eyes grew accustomed to the dark she noticed the bulky form of the midwife, herself dressed in clothes as black as night, at the big chest in the corner of the room.

"Annie," Sally whispered loudly.

Annie lumbered across to the doorway.

"How is she?"

"Asleep," said Annie.

"Is that good?" wondered Sally.

Annie shook her head. "Any sign of the boyos?"

"Oh. You mean Mr Stewart? No, not yet."

Annie shook her head again.

"Would you like something? A cup of tea?"

She never said no to a cup of tea, and drank about twenty a day. So Sally went back downstairs and made a pot. She had delivered her refreshment to Annie, and given some tea to Douglas and Jane, and peeled a basin of potatoes for dinner, when at last William Stewart arrived with the doctor.

The doctor was a large, blowsy man: a male version of Annie Borland. The rule seemed to be that all medical practitioners were fat, red in the face, and short of breath. He was obviously better off than Annie, however: his suit was well-cut, his white shirt gleaming, and he had a heavy gold chain dangling from his breast pocket. On his head was a high top-hat. Sally wondered how he had managed it on horseback, until she caught sight of his trap in the yard.

He removed the high hat and placed it on one of the kitchen chairs, before going upstairs to examine the patient. William Stewart did not accompany him but stayed down with Sally, his head buried in the weekly newspaper. Sally caught a glimpse of the name "Parnell" on the front page, and would have very much liked to know what the latest story of the Irish Party leader was but did not dare to ask. Instead, she put the potatoes on to boil and informed William Stewart that she was going to collect Emily from school. This was not a necessary part of her routine, since Emily was quite well able to come home from school alone. But Sally felt she had to get out of the house, if only for half an hour. She told William that the dinner would be ready when she came home, and let him know that his two younger children were in the yard and would need to be supervised from time to time in her absence.

Sally began to walk listlessly along the narrow road that wound past the Stewarts' farm and on through the wide, shallow valley. The events of the past few days had tired her more than she had realised and she felt cold and exhausted. It was a grey day, dull and very cold. The fields looked bald and sullen, the hedges ragged. "How miserable everything is!" she said, aloud. Her voice drifted wearily into the bleak hedgerows. There was no answer from them or from the grass or from the wind that whipped at her nose and ears. Tears pricked her eyes. She wanted to be at home. She wanted to sit with her mother by her own fireside, and tell her everything. She wanted to sit beside Maura in school, and write essays and giggle. She wanted to dance with Manus.

Her tears began to flow hot and fast. She sat down on a stone at the roadside, and sobbed as if her heart would break.

She was so busy crying that she did not hear a heavy footstep approaching. Suddenly, a large warm hand was patting her shoulder, and a deep voice saying, "What's the matter with ye? What's the matter?"

She looked up at the round red face of Robert Campbell.

Then she looked down again.

"Feeling lonesome, eh?" he asked, softly. "Or are they not treatin' you well over at Stewarts'?"

It was a full minute before Sally could manage to reply. He waited patiently.

"No, it's not...it's not that," she said. "They treat me very well. It's just that it's all been so dreadful during the last few days. Mrs Stewart has had this baby and she's not well, and William is drinking, and I don't know what's going to happen."

"I see. I see," said Robert Campbell. He put his enormous arm around Sally's shoulder. "It's a lot of responsibility for a wee girl like you, the running of that household. It's all too much, I'll warrant. You'll have Annie Borland there with you?"

"She's been tending Mrs Stewart. But I don't know how long she's going to stay."

"No. No, I suppose you don't. Where are you off to now?"

"I'm going to the school, to collect Emily."

"Maybe you could do with an afternoon off?"

"How can I do that? There's nobody to mind the children, or cook, or do anything over there. He's not there half the time..."

"Is he there now?"

"Yes. I told him he'd have to stay, while I was getting Emily. I'd better hurry up, she'll be out..."

Sally shook off his arm and began to walk.

"Listen, wait a wee minute. I'll tell you what, what do you think of this? I'll go to the school and fetch the wee girl, and you drop in to our place and have a chat with your sister. You'd like that, wouldn't you?"

"Well, yes," said Sally, whose tears had dried up by now. She was feeling almost calm again.

"Right you are, then. I'll bring the wee girl home and have a talk with young William. It's time somebody had, by the sounds of things."

"All right," said Sally, feeling light-hearted again, at the prospect of seeing Katie. "Thank you. You are very kind."

"Och, don't you mention it," said Robert Campbell.

14

Pishogues

Robert Campbell came into his house with Sally and told his mother that Katie should have a few hours free to spend with Sally. "They're going to walk into Ballygowl and buy finery for themselves!" he said, with a wink at Sally.

"Och, nothin' can surprise me anymore!" said the old woman. Her voice sounded like a wheel that needs oiling. "Let them buy all the finery they want, furs and feathers and why don't they paint their faces while they're at it? Strumpets is what all the young ones are nowadays, strumpets!"

She spat into the fire. It hissed a long, slow response.

"Off you go, girls," said Robert, opening the door for them. As Sally passed, he pressed a coin into her hand. The coin felt thick and smooth. It must be a florin. They would be able to get something to eat, at least, if they did go to the village. And if not, it would come in handy for something else. Sally had already felt that one of the many problems in her life at the moment was her complete lack of cash. She was literally penniless. Her wages would be paid to her when her six months were up, not a day earlier. In the meantime, she had nothing with which to buy a handful of sweets, or a ribbon for her hair. Or with which, she thought cynically, to escape. That was the difference between having an ordinary job and being "hired." If you get paid once a week, you can quit without losing anything. If Sally quit, she would forfeit all the money she had earned until then.

"Goodbye," she said to Robert, with genuine gratitude. Katie was still wrapping herself up in her thick shawl, and she left the house wordlessly.

"What's all this about?" she asked, her eyes wide with surprise, as soon as the rusty gate had clanged shut behind them. "My eyes nearly popped out of my head when I saw you coming in the door with Rob Roy!"

Sally explained.

"He's very kind, isn't he?"

"He's not the worst," agreed Katie, thoughtfully. "Although I still don't trust him fully."

"You think he's going to jump on you or something?" scoffed Sally. Katie was turning into such a bag of nerves.

"Sometimes I do. But the more I get to know him the more I feel he'll not do anything about it. He's not bad, really. Just a bit fed up."

"So everything is all right with you, then?"

"It'd be all right if the old woman wasn't stark raving mad," said Katie. "But she is; she's totally loony. The neighbours are saying she's a witch and turns herself into a hare in the early morning to steal their milk."

"If you believe that you'd believe anything!" Sally was really scornful this time. "Have you ever seen her transforming into a hare?"

"No, I haven't," said Katie. "But it's not the milking season, is it? So she wouldn't be in business now, would

she? The summer is her busy time, I'm told. She's up bright
and early from May morning on, milking the cows for miles
around. Loads of people have seen her. They've even tried
to shoot her but she always gets away."

"Do you know what? I think it's you who's mad, Katie
Gallagher, not poor Mrs Campbell."

"Honest to God, Sally, I'm telling you. It's just what
Molly Patterson from the next farm told me. She's very
nice; she'd never make up things. And do you know the
proof of it?"

"What?" asked Sally sceptically.

"It's the limp she has. Did you ever notice how she
limps? She's got a bad leg."

"She's old, Katie. Practically every old woman has a bad
leg. Think of our granny. She can't even walk with her
rheumatism."

"You just wait a minute now, till I tell you how she got
that leg. Just hold your horses and I'll tell you. It happened
like this. It was one summer morning, a couple of years
back. Early in the morning, dawn. And she was out as usual,
in the shape of a hare, milking the cows down on one of the
wee farms, McGettigans. And Hughie McGettigan had
known that this was going on. He'd been getting no good
at all from his cows the whole summer. And he'd often seen
the hare amongst them, when he came out to milk them in
the morning. And anyway he decided to get a gun and
shoot the hare. So this morning he was ready waiting. And
she came along and was up on her hind legs, milking. And
he set the dog on her. But she ran anyway and the dog
chased her. And she twisted and turned and twisted and
turned, and still the dog kept after her. He chased her for
about half a mile. Hughie had mounted his horse and was
after the two of them. And at last when it looked as though

she must be tiring, they came to the Campbells' house. The hare gave a great leap and jumped over the gate. And just as she was jumping over it, the hound bit her on the hind leg, on the foot. And then the hare ran on into the house. The door was open.

"Well, Hughie got down off his horse and went up and knocked politely on the door. And old Mrs Campbell answered him. 'Come in,' she said. And in he went. And she was inside, sitting on the chair by the fire, the one she's always in. But her hair was all down around her and she was holding her foot in her hand. It was pouring blood, all over the floor.

"'I'm after cutting myself on the breadknife,' she said. 'I'm bleeding to death, will you ever get me a bandage?'

"'I will indeed,' said he. 'I'll get you a bandage, all right, if you promise never to steal my milk again.'

"She promised. But of course she's still at it, injured foot and all. She won't stop till she dies, so they say. It's in her nature, her witchy nature."

"Sounds very unlikely to me," shrugged Sally. "That's just an old pishogue. I've heard it before, even, I think. I think I've heard them telling some story like that about old Mrs Deeney back home. You must have heard that too?"

"No. I never did." Katie spoke stubbornly. "Even if I did, what difference would it make? Mrs Deeney could be a witch, too. There's lots of them about, you know. Actually, Mrs Deeney reminds me a bit of Granny Campbell. She's the same sort of eyes, those real shiny eyes that sort of see through you."

"Oh, really! That just shows she's got a bit of life in her."

"Come on, Sally. You've seen her, at her pots and pans. She's always stirring up things, making concoctions. Ferrets' leavings, she had me looking for the other day. She was making a cure for measles. Other times she wants a dead mouse or the tongue of a fox."

"But that's all for cures. It's medicine," protested Sally.

"Not proper medicine. Not like the doctor."

Sally thought of the doctor.

"No, not like him," she agreed. "More like Annie Borland."

"Annie Borland?" It was Katie's turn to be puzzled.

"The midwife. She's been nursing Mrs Stewart. She's wonderful, I like her a lot."

"Well if she's wonderful she's not like Granny Campbell. For heaven's sake, you heard her calling us strumpets. She's cracked as an old skittle. I'm telling you. She's always going on about Kitty O'Shea, the English strumpet, as she calls her. She seems to have got her on the brain."

"I thought she was glad that Parnell was in trouble."

"Oh she is, she is. But she still can't stand Kitty O'Shea. I don't know why, really. I mean, she should be grateful to her, since she doesn't want Home Rule."

"People are funny. They don't always think straight."

"They don't, do they?"

For a few minutes they walked along in silence. Then Sally spoke.

"Well, what'll we do? Do you fancy going into Ballygowl, as he suggested, or what?"

"What else is there to do? Unless we run away?"

The two sisters looked at one another. Their eyes grew bright when they thought of being at home again. They clutched one another's arms.

Then Sally pulled away.

"I can't go," she said. Her voice was small and sad. "Apart from anything else, I can't go and leave the Stewarts in the lurch. The mistress is so bad at the minute, I hate to think of what would happen to the children if I walked out now."

"They'd manage, Sally, don't you worry about them. Sure they've lots of money. No matter what happens, they'll manage."

"No," said Sally, thinking of Emily, whom she had begun to respect over the last couple of days. She was such a good, patient little one. And Jane was sweet. Even Douglas she had grown more tolerant of, although he was not good or patient or sweet. Maybe she liked him because he was none of those things.

"The poor little brats. Think of how they feel: their mother is dangerously ill, their father is drinking like a fish. They've been as brave as brave. Emily especially. She understands exactly what's going on and she's very close to her mother but she never cries or makes a nuisance of herself. She has to act like a child about twice her age. I feel really sorry for her. I mean, I used to think if you had loads of money and a father and mother and all that that you would be perfectly happy. But now I see that it's not like that. They're having an awful time, just now anyway. I just can't leave them. As well as that, I don't want to go home without any wages. Mammy needs the money, that's what she sent us here for."

Katie gazed at Sally, awestruck. Who would have believed that her harum-scarum sister, Selfish Sally, as she had often called her privately, could be so considerate! Katie was supposed to be the unselfish one, always thinking of others, never of herself. The tables seemed to have turned. After a few weeks of being away from home, Sally had grown up and Katie had reverted to childishness. She couldn't help it. She just couldn't bear being away from home.

"Oh Sally! I don't know how I'll stick it for five more

months!"

"Four, soon, it's nearly Christmas," said Sally.

"Christmas! What a Christmas!"

"Well, we can get ourselves a Christmas present now today, in Ballygowl. That's what we can do. And Katie!"

"Yes?"

"Remember what I said to you before. If you're ever in real trouble, I mean real trouble, not trouble because of stories the neighbours are telling you, come to me, won't you? Just come right over to the Stewarts' place if anything bad really seems to be about to happen. Promise?"

"Of course I promise. You don't think I'd stay in that place for one second if I felt in danger, do you?"

"Well. Don't."

"Or you either, for that matter."

"Oh, I won't be," said Sally, and she realised that it was true. She was perfectly safe at the Stewarts' farm. In fact, she felt more in control of things than anyone else there.

15

Money to Spend

They walked into the village. By the time they reached it, darkness was falling, and the little shops were lit with oil lamps and candles. Some of them were decorated with holly and sprigs of ivy, and had Christmas novelties heaped in the windows. The girls feasted their eyes on pyramids of boiled sweets, orange and pink and green and yellow, on rich coffee-coloured sticks of Peggy's Leg, on boxes of expensive chocolate, gaily adorned with large ribbons and pictures of beautiful ladies, strolling in romantic gardens. They looked in the draper's shop, admiring the dresses and coats and hats which hung there and wishing they could exchange their shabby clothes for them.

"I'd love a hat like that," said Sally wistfully, pointing to a low-crowned, flat-brimmed felt hat, all the fashion at that time. It was dark green in colour, and had a dark purple and white ribbon around the brim.

"A cat may look at a king," said Katie. "People like us don't wear hats." She pulled her red shawl closer around her ears. It was getting very cold.

"No, they don't," said Sally. "But Mrs Stewart does, for

instance. She has a black bonnet for kirk on Sundays and a grey hat that she wears sometimes when she comes here to go shopping. If she can wear a hat, why can't I? We're not all that different."

"Different enough," said Katie, with a dry laugh. "She's your mistress, remember. She's the wife of a big farmer. You're just the hired girl."

"But our father is...was a farmer, too."

"A little farmer, on a little farm in a little valley in Donegal. There is a difference."

"Yes, I suppose you're right," sighed Sally. "I feel rich now, with all this money, though. So why shouldn't I wear whatever I feel like?"

"You don't want that hat, Sally." She tugged her sister by the arm. "Why don't we go into that little shop across the way and have something to eat? I'm starving. We can finish our shopping afterwards."

They crossed the road and entered a shop named "Stewarts" (many people in the area were called by this name). It had flitches of bacon hanging in the window and baskets piled with eggs in front of the counter. As well as being a grocers it was a public house. Katie asked if they could have something to eat and the woman behind the counter said yes: they could have a plate of peas or some scones. The girls decided on the scones, and with them a glass of raspberry cordial. There was one rickety table in a corner at the back of the shop, and they sat there sipping their ruby-coloured drinks, observing the goings-on of the establishment with interest. As well as the woman, who had disappeared and was, presumably, preparing their food, there was a boy assistant. He was very fat, wrapped in a tobacco-coloured coat so tightly that he resembled a big cigar. He was engaged in cutting an enormous block of butter into pound pieces, wrapping them in greaseproof paper and building a wall of them on a shelf behind the counter. He carried out his work with great care and at the slowest imaginable speed. Sally ached to do it herself: it was so painful to watch him. After a few minutes a customer came in, a farmer's wife who wanted to buy the ingredients for her Christmas brack. The complications of this order seemed to drive the boy into a frenzy. The customer appeared to know his ways and repeated everything in a loud, slow voice about six times. But still he scratched his head and couldn't remember whether she wanted two pounds of raisins and three lemons or three raisins and two pounds of lemons. Her voice got higher and higher, and the pace of it speeded up considerably, until finally the woman, the boy's mother, it seemed, appeared. She placed a big plate of scones, steaming hot and dripping with butter, in front of the girls and went to the rescue of the customer with a "Hold on there now, Mrs Carr, I'll look after that for you. Off you go, Billy, and cut that butter, like a good lad."

The girls ate their snack with relish. It was absolutely delicious, exactly what they needed. Afterwards, they both felt replete and happy. They paid the woman the cost of the meal, sixpence for the two of them, and bought a bar of chocolate to eat on the way home. They had already said goodbye when Sally caught sight of something that made her start in surprise: a small bookcase, full of books. It was behind two sacks of flour just inside the door. The sacks had hidden it from view, but when she was opening the door she suddenly noticed it.

"Goodness me, books!" she said, in astonishment.

"Yes dear," said the woman, smiling at her. "That's our wee library."

"Library? You mean...they're for sale?"

"No. It's a lending library. You pay so much and you borrow a book for two weeks. Then when you've read it you leave it back."

"And if you're late you pay again!" said the other woman, the one who was going to make a cake.

"Hm!" Sally forgot to be shy, she was so fascinated by this idea. "I've never come across anything like that before. It's a great idea, isn't it? Lots of people get to read the same book. How much does it cost, to borrow one?"

"Tuppence a time."

"Tuppence! It's a lot."

"All those books cost more than a shilling each, I'll have you know. Some of the real big ones cost two-and-sixpence. We have to eat, you know."

"Oh yes, I don't mean that it's unreasonable. I just mean tuppence would be a lot for me."

Katie, who was getting tired standing in the doorway, with the cold dark night nipping at her legs and her nose, said:

"One won't break us. Why don't you borrow one now? We have plenty of money for the moment."

This was, of course, just what Sally wanted to do. She hadn't had a single new book to read in weeks. She was starving for one.

"Well...do you think...?"

"Yes, of course. Go ahead, be nice to yourself. See if there's something there you'd like."

Sally stooped down and began to examine the books. There were none that she recognised, but they all looked interesting. There were lots by someone called LT Meade, with illustrations of rich little girls at school. She picked one called _The Little Princess of Tower Hill_ because it was the thickest book on the shelves. Experience had taught her that slim books were not a good idea, for her.

The shopkeeper, Mrs Stewart, wrote down Sally's name and address in a black ledger labelled "Stewart's Library: Register of Borrowers." She wrote slowly and laboriously, but she was educated. Sally knew this, because she was able to spell the name LT Meade and the title of the novel without looking at it more than once. Of course, she was probably accustomed to writing out the names of all the books very often, since there were not more than thirty in the entire library.

"That'll be twopence, please, then," she said, looking at Sally rather grimly, as if she suspected her of not having the money.

Sally handed over the required sum.

"And it must be back here two weeks from today, without fail. Otherwise there is a fine of a penny for every week it's overdue."

"I understand," said Sally, wondering how she would get back to Ballygowl in two weeks' time. "I'll be back, don't worry."

And she went out into the wintry street, hugging her book to her chest in delight.

Katie bought a halfpenny toffee bar for herself and stuck it in her pocket. Sally tried to persuade her to get something else, but she refused point blank to do so. "There'll be other days!" she said. "I know there will."

They walked briskly back to the Campbell cottage. Sally left Katie at the gate, with a hug and a promise to call over in a few days' time. Then she skipped and ran all the way "home," which was how she was beginning to refer to the Stewarts' farm in her innermost thoughts.

16

Missing!

When Sally got back to the farmhouse, she found it in a terrible state. Emily and Jane were in the kitchen, huddled together close to the fire which had almost gone out. The table was piled with dirty crockery. Even the basket of potatoes and skins, left over from the midday dinner, was still sitting in the middle of it. Some tattered mud-coloured skins littered the stained white cloth. Nobody had lit the lamp, although by now it was quite dark. All in all, an air of acute disorder reigned.

Emily jumped to her feet when Sally walked in, and ran over to her. Impulsively Sally opened her arms and gave her a hug. Jane sidled more slowly across the floor. For a few moments, the two little girls clung to the housemaid, the only person to have shown them any affection at all in more than a week. Sally held them tightly, recognising their need for warmth. Poor little things! They were completely lost without their mother.

"Where is Douglas?" she asked, when the girls seemed to be feeling happier, and had loosened their hold on her.

"We don't know," said Emily quickly.

"He runned away," added Jane.

"We told Father but...but..."

"He told us to run way too. But we didn't, did we Em'ly? We don't want to run way cause it's too cold out and it's goin' to rain."

"When did this happen?" Sally was alarmed. "And..." She postponed her second question until the first should be answered.

"Hours ago. Soon after dinner," said Emily. "He just walked off. I thought he might be going out to play outside but I checked after a while and he wasn't there."

"Papa smacked him," said Jane. "Papa smacked him because he was making too much noise and annoying poor Mamma. So he runned away. I knowed he runned away but Em'ly wouldn't b'lieve me, she wouldn't b'lieve me, sure you didn't Em'ly?"

"And where is your father?" asked Sally.

"He was upstairs with Mamma until half an hour ago," said Emily. Her little face was white. "Then he went off to get the doctor. She's worse, I think."

"What about Annie Borland?"

"She's not here. She went off with the baby this morning," Emily was tearful. "Looking for a nurse, or something like that."

Sally looked at the two little girls.

"Listen," she said. "I want you two to stay right here. Do you understand?"

They nodded solemnly.

First Sally dashed upstairs. The sickroom was in total darkness. She lit the bedside candle and looked at Mrs Stewart. Her face was a dead yellow colour, and her skin looked dry as an almond skin. Her once shining hair lay in a dull matted web across the pillow. But her eyes were closed and she was breathing steadily. Sally sighed in relief.

She settled the white sheet over the patient's chest, and left the room quietly but speedily. Pausing only to kiss the girls and remind them to stay inside, she left the house.

As soon as she stood at the gate of the farmyard, the enormity of the task she was undertaking dawned on her. All around the countryside lay, not completely dark, it is true, but glinting frostily in the light of a half-moon. Trees and bushes shivered, strange black monsters, in the icy fields. A few weak lights glittered here and there in the wide valley. The utter silence of the country night was broken by the other-worldly screams of a fox in the far-off woodland. The whole landscape seemed huge and hostile, full of dangerous traps for a small boy on his own. Where, in such a place, could you begin to search?

She began to walk slowly along the road. Probably Douglas would have done that, when running away. Other possibilities, such as that he might have struck out across the fields towards the quarry, in which there was a black lake that was said to be bottomless, or that he would have tried to find the railway track with the intention of catching a train, were too terrifying to consider. Better believe, for a start, that he had begun to walk to Ballygowl. In that case, why hadn't she and Katie met him at some stage on their walk? But there had been the half-hour or so when she had called for Katie; there had been the hour or more they had spent in Ballygowl, in the shop. He could have been on the road at either of those times. They could easily have missed him. And then, could he have managed to walk the whole way to the town? It was unlikely. Much more likely that he had grown tired, sat down in a haystack or at the side of the road, perhaps called into some house along the way. If that had happened, wouldn't the owners have brought him home? Well, maybe that had just happened...

Weighing the possibilities, Sally moved along, keeping her eyes on the ditch as she went. What she would have to do, she realised, was get help. And there was only one place in which to ask for that. As quickly as she could, she made her way to the Campbells' cottage.

Katie answered her knock.

"Goodness gracious, Sally, what are you doing here?" she exclaimed in astonishment when she opened the door.

Sally explained quickly.

Luckily Robert was at home. He got up from his fireside seat and donned his greatcoat immediately.

"Come on, Katie," he said, "you'd better help in this search too. It'll not be easy, finding a young lad at this time of night. But we have to find him."

He did not need to state why. Katie wrapped herself in her big red shawl, and the threesome left the cottage, saying goodbye offhandedly to old Granny Campbell, who was sitting by the fire, humming to herself and knitting a sock.

"Now," said Robert Campbell, as soon as they were in the garden. "We'll both take torches"—he nodded at Sally—"and search the road and the ditches between here and Ballygowl. And you," he nodded at Katie, "go you over to the McElhinneys' farm and let them know. Tell them to get all hands out immediately. You mind where they live?"

"Aye," said Katie. She set off. Robert went into a ramshackle stable at the side of the house and emerged with two long wooden torches. The flickering flames provided a certain amount of light, and would make the job of searching much easier than it had been for Sally, relying on the light of the moon.

"You take the left side of the way and I'll take the right," he said, "and we'll walk to Ballygowl."

They did so. They looked in every ditch and every field by the wayside. When they came to the wood, which was manageably small, they entered it and searched under every tree. All the time, Robert Campbell called at the top of his lungs "Doug-las, Doug-las!" At first Sally was self-conscious about shouting in this style, with him so near at hand. But she soon forgot about her shyness and yelled as loudly as she could.

It took them about an hour and a half to reach Ballygowl. Still no sign of Douglas.

"Now, what we'll do is go to every house and enquire after him. And if we can't find him we'll ask the whole town to come out and search."

They began to knock on doors, Sally taking one side of the street and Robert the other. At every door, she was greeted by questioning, then sympathetic, faces. But never by Douglas's face. They tried every single house in the town but he was not there. There was not, however, any need to ask the townspeople to help them. Everyone knew the Stewarts, and everyone, it seemed, thought wee Douglas Stewart was the finest wee boy who had ever been born in the history of the world. Within minutes there were thirty or forty men, many carrying torches, on the street. Robert Campbell took charge of the group. He divided it up into clusters of four, and allocated specific areas to each cluster. When the last of the groups had set off, he turned to Sally.

"Now, wee lass, you look exhausted. You've done more than enough for today. Why don't you go home and go to your bed?"

Sally protested. But he placed his big hand on her shoulder and said, "The two wee girls need looking after too."

"Their father should be home by now," said Sally, but

without much conviction.

"Maybe and maybe not. You better get back there, anyway. For your own sake and for theirs. Half the country is out looking for that wee lad, there's no need for you to be in on the search now. Anyhow, this kind of thing is no work for a girl."

Sally resented that, in one way. In another, it was refreshing to be treated as a real girl, who could get tired. Hired girls were usually treated as if they were just as tough as men by the people who employed them. It was only rich girls and women who were supposed to be delicate and feminine.

She said goodbye and left.

She was, as he had said, exhausted. This was the fourth time she had walked the three miles between Ballygowl and the Stewart farm. Her feet felt heavy as lead, as she trudged along the cold gloomy road. Her mind was so weary that she did not have the energy to be worried. Everything was as bad as could be, it seemed, and could hardly get worse. She felt that if the bottom fell out of the world and she dropped down into hell she would shrug her shoulders and think, "Who cares?" All she wanted to do was to lay her head on her pillow and lose consciousness in sleep.

She walked so slowly that the journey home took almost an hour. It felt like about ten. Although Sally had been saying to herself that she was numb to any new feelings, when she at last caught sight of the light in the kitchen window of the farm, she felt a surge of relief flood her body. With renewed energy she trod the last steps to the gate of the farm.

Just as she was passing the pigsty, which was just inside the outer gate, she heard a muffled sound. Probably the old sow stirring in her sleep...but perhaps...perhaps. Sally had an intuition. Something told her that the sound had not been made by a pig. She went and pushed the door of the sty.

It would not open.

She pushed harder, and it still wouldn't open.

Then she began to hammer on it with her fists.

If Douglas was inside, why didn't he cry out, or otherwise let her know that he was there?

She thrust the whole weight of her body against the door, and gave a mighty shove.

It gave way. She almost fell into the pigsty.

Her torch had gone out and for a minute she could see absolutely nothing. The dark was fragrant with the smell of pig, and warm with pig-heat, and she could hear the old sow now, breathing heavily from her bed of straw.

After a minute or so, the shapes and forms began to develop.

She could make out the tiny closed window, and the fence that railed off the centre of the sty from the outer passage. She could make out the shape of the sow, huge as a horse, lying in the straw. And she could see, huddled against the soft, hot side of the old motherly pig, the shape of a small boy.

He was fast asleep, and snoring softly like a tiny piglet.

Sally's eyes filled with tears as she looked at him.

Tears of relief, at having found him, safe and in one piece. And tears of pity, for the poor little child who had run to a pig for comfort.

As quietly and gently as she could, she entered the stall and picked him up from his cosy bed. It seemed almost a pity to move him from where he was so comfortable. But he was in a certain amount of danger: if the sow rolled on top of him, she could smother him, as she often did smother

her own piglets. Carefully, Sally carried Douglas out of the sty and across the farmyard to the house. As the cold night air hit him, he opened his eyes sleepily.

"It's only me," said Sally softly. "You go back to sleep. Good little boy, good little boy!"

And he did.

17

Lady of the House

Sally was relieved to see that William Stewart was in the house when she came in. He was seated at the table, leaning intently across the remains of the dinner, talking to the doctor. When Sally walked in carrying her small human burden, he glanced up in surprise. She motioned him to stay silent and carried Douglas upstairs, where she laid him in bed alongside Jane: she did not want him to sleep alone that night of all nights.

Downstairs, William jumped up and clasped her hand. It was the first time he had made a warm human gesture towards her. He said very little and when she had told him her story he asked her to sit down at the table with himself and the doctor.

"Capital that you found the young lad, absolutely capital!" began the latter, his brilliant red face wearing its typically cheerful grin.

"Yes but do you realise that half the country is out searching for him?" interrupted Sally. "We'll have to let them know…"

"Yes, yes—" The doctor gestured impatiently—"We'll see to that presently. For the moment we've got to tell you something else."

Sally felt her stomach sink. She couldn't take any more. Not tonight. She couldn't.

"Mrs Stewart is very ill. Seriously ill, I'm afraid," said the doctor trying to make his comical face look suitably solemn. And failing. "She's going to have to be moved to hospital."

"Hospital?" Sally was aghast. She had never heard of anyone going to hospital before. It sounded to her like the next best thing to the graveyard.

"She will go to hospital in Derry, to have an operation."

Oh God, thought Sally. Poor Mrs Stewart! But she remained silent.

"Tomorrow, we're thinking of moving her. Without this operation, she has no chance."

And with it? Sally did not voice the question but her mind lingered on a picture of the doctor wielding a long sharp knife. She wouldn't like to be at his mercy.

"She has a kidney problem. So she's for the knife and it's off she'll have to go."

The doctor couldn't resist half a smile which he suppressed as fast as he could.

"Derry's a long way off," Sally said distantly, not noticing his lapse of taste.

"Aye, it is that," said William Stewart, speaking for the first time. His voice sounded weary. "And I'll have to go with her. That's why I'm talking to you, Sally. I'm leaving you in charge here until I come back. I know you can manage it and anyway I have no one else."

"Mm," said Sally doubtfully. No one else? What about his family? Her family? Everyone had relations, hadn't they?

"My mother and father are dead," he said, reading her thoughts. "And she has only her father, who's not much good with wee ones." He smiled. "So there is nobody. You'll not have to worry about the farm, of course. Just look after the children, as you have been doing, until I get back."

"And when will that be?"

"In two weeks at the earliest," said the doctor. "It could be longer. Yes. It could be longer."

"Annie Borland has found a nurse for the baby," William went on quickly. "You won't have to bother about her either. It'll just be the three older ones. And Robert Campbell will keep an eye on things around here. You should be able to manage."

"All right," said Sally. She felt too tired to think about what all this meant. Her mind was blank and the only thing she wanted to do was sleep. "All right," she said. "I think I'll be able to manage." She stood up. "And now," she yawned, "if you'll excuse me, I'll go to bed. I've had a very long day and I'm tired. I'll see you in the morning."

"Aye, aye," said William Stewart, in the same dispirited tone. "Goodnight, then."

"Goodnight," said the doctor, with a smile wrinkling up his large red face. "Sleep well."

Sally turned at the foot of the stairs.

"You're not forgetting the search-party, are you?"

Both faces looked vacant for a second.

"Och no," said William Stewart. "I'm away now to light a bonfire to let them know the lad is home safe. I think I might even have a flare or two to fire up. That should give them the message as well as anything."

And he rose shakily to his feet.

Sally trudged up the wooden stairs. Really, he had made very little fuss about Douglas. She wondered if he realised what had happened at all. Well, the man had a lot on his plate at the moment. Perhaps he could be forgiven for not paying much attention to the fact that his son had been lost all day and had just now been saved. Maybe he had guessed that Douglas would turn up safe and sound—that it wasn't worth worrying too much about him.

When Sally came downstairs the following morning William Stewart was already up and making preparations for the journey. Mrs Stewart would be taken in the back of a cart to Ballygowl where they would catch the train to Derry.

The cart stood outside the kitchen door. William had placed a mattress, pillow and blankets in it. All that remained to be done was to harness the horse and to carry Mrs Stewart and settle her in the makeshift bed.

"Lucky it's not raining," said Sally. In fact it promised to be a bright sunny day although it was not yet fully light.

William grunted in reply.

Sally busied herself with the kettle and the breakfast porridge, and then went to call the children. She wondered how Mrs Stewart would be carried down but did not like to ask. By the time she had dressed Douglas and got the family started on breakfast she found out. Robert Campbell and the doctor arrived on the scene, the latter looking very dishevelled, as if he had slept in his clothes. The three men ascended the stairs and in a short time returned again. William and Robert carried Mrs Stewart, who seemed to be asleep, and the doctor came behind blustering and shouting warnings to them to watch where they were going and mind not to hit the ceiling. The children and Sally stared in shock at the scene. Mrs Stewart, who was wrapped in a white woolly blanket from head to toe, had a face the colour of lemon jelly. Her eyes were closed and her lips, white and thin, hung half-open.

"Mamma!" screamed Douglas and rushed towards her.

The eyes did not open. Sally ran and clasped Douglas in her arms, kissing his head and face. He shivered, frightened and hurt, but did not cry. The two girls made no attempt to approach their mother but gazed at her, numbed with horror. They all went to the window and watched as the patient was laid in the cart and covered with more quilts and blankets so that eventually nothing was visible but a large white mound. Sally then waited for William Stewart to return to the kitchen and issue some last instruction or say goodbye to the children. But no such thing occurred. He stepped up on the driver's box and the doctor got up beside him. With a curt "Gee-up!" they were off, the horse walking slowly and steadily across the yard and out the gate which Robert Campbell held open.

"Now, back and finish your breakfast!" said Sally to the children, as if what they had witnessed was perfectly normal. "Emily will be late for school if we don't hurry up!"

Just as she was ready to send Emily off, Robert Campbell came in. He picked up Douglas and swung him high in the air.

"So you were sleeping with the old sow yesterday, were ye, young man? How do you feel after that?"

"The same," said Douglas solemnly.

"The same? The same as the pigs, do you mean?"

"The same as before," said Douglas crossly. He hated to be deliberately misunderstood by grown-ups who were trying to laugh at him. Emily and Jane, however, grinned happily. Even Emily had her little weakness: she enjoyed seeing Douglas being teased.

"When you're booking into the pigsty in future, please keep us informed," said Robert. "You never know, somebody else might like to bed down there too. It's not fair to hog all the space. Do ye get the joke? Hog the space, ha, ha, ha!"

Sally grinned, amazed. It was not often that Robert Campbell made jokes. The girls giggled in delight.

"Here, wee Emily, are you off to school? I'll walk over the road with you. Sally here has plenty on her hands today. If you need any help, by the way, send over to me for it, won't you? Maybe I'll get that sister of yours to come over and lend you a hand after dinner. Would you like that?"

"Oh yes," said Sally. "That would be very helpful. Thank you very much."

"Och, don't mention it!" said Robert. And he went off, leading Emily by the hand.

There was a great deal of work to be done, cleaning the kitchen and tidying the house. Nobody had bothered about it for days. There was a mountain of dishes to be washed. Clothes lay all over the place. There were buckets of milk which hadn't been skimmed or poured into jugs. And, as Sally realised, much else besides. She set Douglas and Jane to draw pictures at the table and busied herself with the housework. The time flew by and before she knew it, Emily was coming in the front door, red and smelling of wind and outdoors.

"Now," said Sally, "after dinner I want you three to go for a walk. Just for the exercise. I can't go with you because I'm expecting my sister to call."

To her surprise they agreed immediately to her suggestion and when their plates were washed they set off. Sally washed up and made herself a cup of tea, something she did not usually have after her dinner. Now, however, she was the lady of the house in a manner of speaking and might as well enjoy whatever privileges there were. She took the cup of tea into the parlour, a room she had never entered before except occasionally to dust. It was a large room, furnished with a suite consisting of a bulging sofa and armchairs which were covered with flowery chintz and bedecked with lace antimacassars. There was a china cabinet in one corner, filled with china cups and saucers and all kinds of delightful ornaments, and in the fireplace was a large brass fan instead of a fire. The walls were painted pink on the top half and brown on the bottom, and over the fireplace was a huge picture of a stag standing on top of a brown hill, looking shocked. Sally guessed that they had won the picture at a carnival. She had often seen ones like it on the hoopla stall.

She sat in one of the big armchairs and began to sip her tea. Although it was cold in the room she felt very happy to be there. It was, in her opinion, the very height of elegance. She would give anything to have a room like this of her own, a room in which she could spend a part of every day, drinking tea, talking to friends or reading. It would be great to have Maura here or one of the other girls from school. And she hadn't even remembered to bring her library book with her this afternoon. Her reading was confined to her bedroom and the late hours of the evening, so she did not even consider doing it downstairs. Some other time, she thought. Her eyes were fixed on the gap in the lace curtains through which she had a glimpse of the farm gate.

She was still sitting there an hour later, daydreaming. Her tea was half-gone and cold, and she herself was quite cold too. Katie had not appeared. Through the gate came the three children, home from their walk, and Robert Campbell. Sally ran into the kitchen quickly and threw a few sods of turf on the fire, which had gone very low.

"Hello!" she said cheerily to the children as they trooped in. "Did you have a nice walk?"

"Yes," answered Emily. "Quite nice. We walked all the way over to Campbells', actually."

"Really?" said Sally. "Did you see my sister? She hasn't come here."

"No, we didn't see her," said Emily. "They thought she was here already. They asked us if we'd met her on the road, coming over to see you. But we hadn't. At least, we didn't think we had. Of course, we've never seen your sister. But we couldn't remember meeting anyone. Only we were not sure."

"Oh dear," said Sally, really very worried. "What can have happened to her?"

"Perhaps we should look in the pigsty," said Emily in her serious voice.

Sally gave her a sharp look. "She must have got lost," she said, not very convincingly.

"I suppose so," said Emily, politely. "Maybe she'll come along any moment now."

But the next person to come in was Robert Campbell.

"Hello, there," he said, cheerfully. "I've come for Katie; it's time she was going back home."

Sally looked at him in dismay. He was leaning against the doorpost, smiling in his quiet genial way, quite oblivious of the fact that Katie had…disappeared.

"Oh yes?" she said, in what she wanted to sound a surprised tone. "Katie? She isn't here, I'm afraid."

"What do you mean, she isn't here?"

"She isn't here. I waited for her all afternoon but she never came."

Campbell moved closer to Sally and scrutinised her face carefully. Under such an examination she felt nervous and hot and hoped she wasn't blushing.

"Is that the truth?" he asked.

"It is," she said simply. "I don't know where she is. Maybe she got lost."

"On the way from my place to here? You must be joking."

"Or maybe she's run away." Sally decided to make a clean breast of it. "She wasn't very happy. With your mother. She was nervous about her. She was, in fact, afraid of her. I asked her to come to me if she ever needed...help. But she hasn't come to me. Maybe she's run away."

Robert Campbell gritted his teeth.

"If so, she won't run far," he said. With that he left the house.

18

A Letter

It was a false alarm. Katie had not run away. She had just gone for a long walk, and forgotten the time, so she didn't manage to call on Sally. When Robert Campbell arrived home, she was in the kitchen, chopping onions and parsley for a stew his mother was preparing for dinner.

Katie is getting more and more unreliable, thought Sally. She doesn't know whether she's coming or going. She's so scatterbrained!

Then she remembered that that's just how she had been herself, before she left home, and laughed. Leaving home certainly changed people.

During the next week, Robert Campbell continued to visit the farm in order to bring in and out the cows morning and evening and to keep an eye on the livestock, as he had promised. Sally milked the few cows that were still yielding and fed the hens and pigs. She did this farmwork while Emily was at school and got some help from Jane and even Douglas, who were happy to oblige, if sometimes less than efficient.

Katie came over almost every afternoon. The idea was

that she should give Sally a hand. But usually they spent the time sitting by the fire, talking, while Emily mixed a cake at the kitchen table and Douglas and Jane played hide-and-seek all over the house.

"It's nice, not having Mamma and Papa here, Sally," Emily said to her, one day. "I miss them. But this is more fun."

"That's just because your mother was sick for the last while. It used to be fun when she wasn't sick."

"Not this much fun," said Emily, taking a cake away from the fire. "She didn't let me cook, or anything."

"Oh well," said Sally, wondering if she really should do this. "It's good that you're having a nice time."

She had to agree with Emily. Life was much much better, without Mrs and Mr Stewart. And everything seemed to be running just as smoothly as before. You'd wonder what all the fuss grown-up people made about running a house or farm was about. Of course, it was a slack time of the year, as far as the farm was concerned. But on the whole everything seemed to work better without the farmer and his wife than with them.

It wasn't perfect. Sometimes, at night, Sally felt lonely and isolated. There was no one with her except the children, from about five o'clock in the evening. The nights were very very long, and Emily tended to get worried about her parents as soon as darkness fell and the wind started to howl around the eaves of the farmhouse. Many days passed and no word came from the Stewarts. Robert Campbell hadn't heard anything, either, and the doctor hadn't appeared since the day he had taken Mrs Stewart to the station. Annie Borland dropped in once, to let Sally know that the baby was thriving with her nurse. But she had no news of the Stewart parents.

"No news is good news," Sally said, when Emily asked about them. And then, not very consistently, she added, "We'll probably get a letter tomorrow."

But two weeks passed and no letter came. Then, one Thursday morning, while Emily was at school and the other two children were eating bread and milk in the kitchen, the postman called with a letter for Sally. It was the very first letter she had received since she had come to Tyrone, and, indeed, the very first letter she had ever received in her life. The hand was a strange one to her, but she guessed, from its strong, rigid lines, that it was William Stewart's.

She opened the letter quickly, with a sense of apprehension, and quickly scanned it. Then, sighing with relief, she read more slowly the brusque but comforting words:

> *Dear Miss Gallagher,*
>
>   *I wish you to tell the children that their mother has had her operation. It was a success, for which they must thank the Lord. Mrs Stewart is making a good recovery. She will remain in Derry until she is well enough to return home, i.e. for three more weeks. I will remain with her.*
>
>   *Check that the black calf's leg is mending and ask Robert Campbell to make sure there is enough fodder in for the next month. I enclose two pounds for Christmas needs.*
>
> *Yours sincerely,*
W Stewart.

When she had absorbed its contents herself, Sally read the letter aloud to Jane and Douglas. They were very pleased with the good news about their mother and even more so by the fact of having had a letter at all. The mention of Christmas, however, disturbed them. They could not imagine that Christmas would come soon and that they would celebrate it without their parents. However, Sally pointed out that as it was already the fifteenth of December that was exactly what was going to happen. She had given no thought at all to the festival, possibly because she did not relish the thought of spending it so far away from her own family. There was little to celebrate. For the sake of the children, however, she would have to do something. She would also have to make contact with her family at home. William Stewart's letter suggested to her the idea of writing a letter herself. Oddly, she had not done so before. The real reason for this was that she would not have considered wasting money on a stamp, which cost three halfpence. A penny-halfpenny which Sally simply had not possessed. But now she had two whole pounds. She could easily spare a few pence for her letter.

Later that day, when Emily had come home from school, she went into the drawing room, and in a big bureau in the corner she found some paper, a pen and a half-full bottle of black ink. It was so long since the ink had been used that the tin lid was stuck fast. She had to get a knife from the kitchen to scrape away the hard black crust of dried ink and then screw the cap with all her might before it would budge. Finally it gave way to her pressure, however, and came away, scattering a few drops over Sally's dress in the process. She was so pleased to have opened the bottle that she paid no attention to the spots. Asking Emily to keep the little ones out of her way, she sat down and dipped the nib into the murky liquid. Luckily the nib seemed new, and she was able to write quite neatly with it.

In her rather beautiful hand, of which she had been proud at school, she penned a long letter to her mother. She told her about Mrs Stewart's illness and the situation in which she now found herself. She closed by asking her mother to write to her as soon as possible and let her know how everyone was at home.

It crossed her mind that she could write to Maura, or Miss Lynch, or Manus, or anyone, if she wanted to. But she decided to put that off for a while. One letter a day was enough.

When it was ready, she rounded up the children and told them she was going to Ballygowl to do some Christmas shopping. Since Douglas and Jane could not walk that far, she decided to drop in to Annie Borland and ask her to keep an eye on them for a few hours. Emily she would take with her, since she deserved a treat of some kind and since she would be able to help, carrying parcels home.

Unfortunately Annie Borland lived in the wrong direction for Ballygowl, but that could not be helped. They walked the quarter of a mile or so to her house across the fields. When they arrived, they were lucky to find her in. She had no objection to minding the children, and they were very happy to stay with her, but Sally found it difficult to get away from her good-humoured but inquisitive questions. She wanted to know everything about the Stewarts, about how Sally was managing at the farm, about Katie and the Campbells. It was very difficult to get her to stop asking questions. Finally, after almost half an hour, Sally and Emily managed to escape from the small, overheated kitchen.

19

Christmas Shopping

Emily was a brisk walker and they covered the three miles to Ballygowl in just over half an hour. Sally's first port of call was the post office, where she stamped and posted the letter to her mother. Then she visited Stewarts' shop and returned her book. Mrs Stewart seemed surprised to see her.

"Did ye read it?" she asked suspiciously, her little beady eyes peering at Sally over the rims of her steel glasses.

"Yes," said Sally. "It's very good. I'll take another one out, if I may."

"It's all the same to me what you take out, alanna," said Mrs Stewart. "As long as you pay, of course."

"Of course," said Sally, coldly, going over to the little bookcase and selecting another volume quickly: there was no addition to the stock since the last time she'd been in. She wondered if anyone else ever borrowed or returned a book. This time she took one called *A Flat Iron for a Farthing. Or some passages in the Life of an Only Son* by JH Ewing. She had never heard of JH Ewing, but she liked the title of the book and there were some nice pictures of children in it. The children were very beautifully dressed and lived in a richly furnished house with a huge garden. They had, according to the illustrations, dozens of wonderful toys, ponies and charming small pet dogs, and there was a tennis court. Sally had never known any child who looked like or lived like the children in this book, or in any other book she had read for that matter. But, perhaps for that very reason, she knew she would enjoy it. The world of the little princess in the last book she had read had been very attractive. At the moment Sally was in the mood for books about rich children with happy lives. She wanted to escape into their wonderful, luxurious world and experience it even at second-hand. Besides, she was rather fond of illustrations, so she had no difficulty in making up her mind that this was the book for her. She gave the shopkeeper her twopence and had the book entered in the register of borrowers. Then she and Emily selected some special foods for Christmas: raisins and oranges, biscuits and sweets, raspberry cordial, bacon and sausages. Even though they bought a lot of food, enough to fill a large box, it all came to less than a pound.

"Can you deliver this to the Stewarts' farm?" asked Sally.

"Oh yes, of course," said Mrs Stewart. "Is the missus still away, so?"

"Yes, she is," said Sally. "I can't carry this home myself."

"We'll send it out to you tomorrow. Will that suit your ladyship?" the shopkeeper spoke kindly, but with a touch of sarcasm. Sally ignored it.

"Tomorrow will be fine," she said. "And now we'd both like lemonade and some scones, please."

"At your service!" said Mrs Stewart. She banged a bell which she had hidden under the counter and her son came quickly in response. Leaving him to mind the shop, she disappeared into the dark interior of her house. Sally and Emily sat down at the single table in the back corner of the shop. Somebody had left a copy of a newspaper, _The Freeman's Journal_, on the table, and Sally glanced at it while she waited. All the news was about Parnell. Apparently he was in serious trouble because of his involvement with Katharine O'Shea and more than half his own party had turned against him.

"I know some who'll be happy about that," said Sally to herself, folding up the paper and leaving it back on the chair where she'd found it, as Mrs Stewart re-emerged from her mysterious room, carrying a tray of tumblers and a big plate of scones. The scones smelled delicious. All that fuss and crisis about Parnell and Home Rule. It seemed to Sally that it had very little to do with real life. With Mrs Stewart, ill in hospital, with Emily, gazing greedily at the plate of scones and for the moment forgetting her problems, with Sally herself, on hire for six months, far away from her family and...well, it was hardly true any more to say "far away from her friends," since she had friends here now. The goings-on of Parnell and Mrs O'Shea and the Irish Party, the question of Home Rule or no Home Rule, seemed so very distant and irrelevant. Would it change life at all, for Emily or Mrs Stewart or Sally? Well, some people, people like Emily's father, seemed to think it would and opposed it for that reason. But what an odd person he was! He seemed to hate life already, even though there was no Home Rule yet anyway. He took no joy in his home or his family, or even in his work. That was why he was always in such bad form. Would he be happier if Parnell and the Irish Party disappeared into the ground, and Ireland was safe and English for evermore? It was hard to imagine that something like that would really change him. But of course you never knew. And worrying about it all obviously gave him an interest in life.

Pushing aside these thoughts, without much difficulty, Sally fell upon the scones. Her appetite was smaller than Emily's. The latter gobbled up three or four scones in quick succession, drained her glass, and then devoured two more scones.

"I mustn't be giving you enough to eat!" gasped Sally in astonishment. Emily was usually rather ladylike in her eating habits and picked delicately at her food.

"I'm really hungry all of a sudden," said Emily, smiling a little guiltily. Her face was red with the effort of so much eating. "It's the long walk, I suppose."

"Yes, that must be it," said Sally. She must remember to make sure she provided some appetising meals for the children over the next few days. It would be awful if they were half-starved, on top of all their other problems.

When they had finished their snack, Sally and Emily crossed the road to the small drapery and haberdashery. The upper floor of the shop had been turned over to toys for the festive season. It was a very tiny floor, and the selection of toys was relatively small. Still, there were dolls, trains, rocking horses, tin soldiers, hoops, balls, and many other things. The girls spent a pleasant hour there, pondering the pros and cons of the various items. In the end, they bought a doll for Jane, a box of soldiers and a small train for Douglas and a painting set for Emily.

"What about you?" asked Emily. "You have to have a present, too."

"Oh no," said Sally. "I'm too big for presents."

She felt, indeed, as if she never wanted a present again. She felt far too serious to be interested in any present that anyone could give her.

Emily, however, insisted. Finally Sally agreed, and, giving Emily two shillings, told her that she could select something for her. Meantime Sally went outside. Five minutes later Emily came out, clutching a paper bag and smiling broadly.

When they all reached the farm, much later, since Annie had invited them to have their tea with her, it was late and very dark. Sally imagined, as she crossed the farmyard, that she heard a slight noise coming from the barn.

"Did you hear that?" she asked the children, in alarm.

The girls shook their heads. Douglas said, "It's the ghost."

"What ghost?"

"The ghost that lives in the barn."

Sally opened the barn door and looked inside. It was too dark to see much but she went right inside and searched as well as she could. She found nothing.

"Probably an owl or something," she said, coming back out. "What's that you were saying about a ghost, Douglas?"

"Huh?" said Douglas, absently. He was busily kicking a stone around the yard.

"The ghost in the barn, silly," said Emily. "When did you see her?"

"I seed her tomorrow," said Douglas. "I seed her lots of times."

"Really? What does she look like?" asked Sally.

"She small an' she got long white hair and she got a horrible face. Really horrible. She got a monster face."

"Hm. What does she wear?" asked Sally, although she was beginning to think that the ghost was another of Douglas's inventions.

"A black dress and a black shawl around her head, that's what she wears," he said convincingly.

"Doesn't she frighten you?"

"Naw, she doesn't frighten me; she stupid."

Sally went over and put her arms around Douglas.

"Douglas," she said. "The next time you see the ghost in the barn, call me. Promise me?"

"All right," said Douglas. "Can I have a bit of bread and jam?"

Douglas had his bread and jam, and milk, in bed, since it was very late. When she had told him and Jane a story and tucked them in, Sally came down and began to tidy up the kitchen. As she was doing so, she noticed crumbs on the table, even though she had cleaned it after dinner and nobody had eaten anything there since.

"Hmm," she said thoughtfully. "Probably Robert Campbell has been in snooping around, when he saw we weren't here."

But she didn't really believe that.

20

The Missing Cake

Early the next morning Robert Campbell came over to milk the cows. Instead of staying out of his way, Sally, who had been looking out for him, went out to the byre and accosted him.

"Good morning, Mr Campbell," she said, sounding braver than she felt. He looked up from Daisy the cow's broad red flank in some surprise. "Hello, Sally," he said, and returned to his milking. For a moment the only sound was the ping of the milk hitting the hard wooden bucket.

Sally continued. "I've been meaning to thank you for your help. I couldn't manage at all without you."

He grunted in reply.

"But there is something else I need to ask you about, too."

The ping stopped.

"It's about your mother. How is your mother, Mr Campbell?"

He looked up.

"She's all right, I suppose. Why do you ask?"

Sally's heart was in her mouth.

"I need to know. Is she at home now, for instance? Do

you know where she is?"

He looked at her between the eyes.

"She was at home when I left this morning," he said. "And as far as I know she's there all the time."

"As far as you know?" went on Sally, feeling more and more nervous. "I think she might be spending some of her time here. And maybe at other houses as well."

"What do you mean?" he asked, his voice grew angry. "Don't give me that old superstition about the milk. She's not taking your milk. Anyway, if it wasn't for me you'd have none at all."

"She's not taking milk. But butter and bread have been disappearing. Food that I leave out for the children is taken before they can eat it. Some clothes are gone. And other things as well, for all I know."

"You are accusing my mother of stealing butter and food and clothing from the Stewarts?" he laughed ironically.

"Somebody is."

"What on earth would my mother want with the Stewarts' bread and butter, or their old clothes? She has more than enough to eat and wear, much more than she needs or wants."

"I know that. But things have been disappearing. I'm sure that it's not the children. I mean, why would they, anyway? Someone else has been visiting the house and taking...borrowing...or stealing, call it what you like. Some intruder."

He looked at her steadily. Daisy turned her head and looked too, with her large doleful eyes, as if wondering why the milking was not progressing normally.

"So you have an intruder. But why suspect my mother?" It was Sally's turn to look quizzical.

"Douglas has seen someone. Someone who, as he

describes her, looks like Mrs Campbell."

Robert Campbell laughed shortly.

"Douglas is a right wee...That child doesn't know whether he's coming or going. Never has since he was a wee baby. Remember the trouble he caused us all just the other week, running off and getting lost like that?" Sally did not know what response she should give to this. She seemed to be getting nowhere with her enquiries. Maybe she was wrong about Mrs Campbell? If so, all she'd succeeded in doing was antagonising Robert, who had been so helpful and kind. It was very hard to know what to do and say, in this kind of situation.

She turned and moved to the door.

"Well," she said, "I suppose I could be wrong. If so, I'm sorry for offending you. But what can I do? It's not very comfortable for me, knowing there's somebody lurking around the farmyard, liable to land in at any moment for all I know. I mean, who do you think it could be? Who on earth could it be?"

And she left the byre. Robert Campbell stared after her for a minute or two, looking dazed. Then he returned to the work in hand, pulling so hard at Daisy that he hurt her.

When he left, about an hour later, Sally checked every one of the outhouses. But she could find no trace of any human being anywhere. She began to wonder if Douglas had been wrong, if she was wrong and if perhaps the children were playing practical jokes on her after all. They were not the prankish kind, they'd been brought up far too strictly for that. But you never could tell. With their parents away they might be changing.

It was now only three days to Christmas. That afternoon, Sally decided to make some preparations. It would cheer everybody up and take their minds off the ghost of the barn, if nothing else.

"First we'll make a cake!" she decided, when the dinner things had been cleared away. "And then we'll make Christmas decorations."

"We never have Christmas decorations," said Emily.

"But you do have presents and a Christmas dinner and all that?"

"Oh yes," she said. "Just no decorations. We think they're..."

She stopped, embarrassed.

"Common?" Sally supplied a word.

Emily nodded.

"Well," Sally wondered for a moment. "Would you like to have them this year?"

All the children cried, "Yes!"

"That's settled then," said Sally firmly. "But first the cake. Jane, you fetch the raisins and flour from the big press. Douglas, you get the wooden spoon..."

They spent a pleasant hour making the cake. When it was mixed in the big yellow bowl, Sally made them all stir the thick dough and make a wish. Finally she stirred it and wished herself.

"What did you wish for? What did you wish for?" Douglas and Jane asked.

"It doesn't come true if you tell," said Sally, placing a warning finger to her lips. She guessed that all the children had wished for the same thing and did not want them to start talking about it. She had noticed that talking about things is sometimes useful, but sometimes it causes trouble. "And now, on with your coats and hats. We're going out to collect holly and ivy in the woods."

"Hurrah!" yelled the children as they ran to get their

coats. Just before they went out, Emily asked:

"But what about the cake, Sally? Don't we have to bake it?"

"It'll take about an hour and a half to cook," said Sally, hopefully. She had never made a cake of this kind before and was not at all sure how long it might take, but she seemed to recall that Christmas bread required a much longer baking time than the everyday variety. "We'll be back by then, just in time to take it off the fire. And then we can paint the ivy berries and decorate the place. It's going to look wonderful!"

They set off in high spirits. The woods were lovely, peaceful and mysterious, a bit like the inside of an empty church. But they were filled with mysterious crackling, crunching sounds.

"You can hear the animals stirring in their sleep!" said Sally, laughing. And it did sound as if hundreds of sleeping squirrels and hedgehogs and bats and other hibernating creatures were constantly tossing and turning—even snoring occasionally. The sounds were probably really made by ice melting and breaking, and by twigs and leaves falling, but it was more interesting to imagine that they had other causes.

The ivy grew around the bigger trees, and the holly in a clump of bushes near the edge of the wood. There were many red berries on the holly: it was a hard winter. The black berries on the ivy seemed to be fewer, but Sally urged the children to pick as many of them as they could. Whitewashed, they would provide a good contrast to the red holly berries.

It was hard work, but after about an hour they had picked as much greenery as they could carry. Then they set out for home. They walked more slowly than they had on the outward journey, since they were tired and laden with their booty. By the time they reached the gate, darkness had fallen, and with it some light flakes of snow.

"It's snowing!" said Emily, her face joyful.

"Hurrah! Hurrah! Hurrah Hurrah Hurrah!" shouted Douglas and Jane in delight.

Sally smiled to herself. She loved snow. But she was concerned that it might bring additional problems. What exactly she did not know. Just the thought of snow made her feel uneasy, however, and she hoped that it would not be a heavy fall.

When they got into the kitchen, the room was filled with a delicious spicy smell. "Hm!" Sally wrinkled up her nose. "That certainly smells done to me."

While the children put away their coats, she went to the pot-oven in which the cake was baking to take it out. But she didn't have to bother. When she got there, the pot was open and the cake gone.

She clapped her hand over her mouth to muffle her scream of dismay. Thinking rapidly, she clapped the oven door shut. Just as she had done so, the children trooped back into the room and over to her side.

"Is it done?" they asked, in unison.

"Not yet," said Sally. "It's a slow one, it's going to take a long time. Let's get busy with the decorations."

She spread the holly and ivy out on the table, and then spent some time searching for whitewash and a brush. She guessed they might be out in one of the outhouses but the last thing she wanted to do was go outside. Finally she found something that would serve the purpose at the bottom of the dresser in the scullery. There was no brush, but she tore up an old rag into strips and gave a bit to each of the children.

"Now, all you have to do is smear each ivy berry with the whitewash. And try not to get it all over yourselves. Then we'll start hanging up the holly and by the time it's up the ivy will be dry."

"What about supper?" asked Douglas. "I's hungry!"

"Goodness, I forgot all about it," said Sally, truthfully. "I'll tell you what, you do the berries while I prepare supper. And after supper we'll do our decorating. And then, bedtime, I think."

Douglas and Jane groaned, although they were so tired that they had already started yawning.

Sally cut some bread and cheese, and filled mugs of milk: it would be a cold supper tonight, even though it was deepest winter. While she was preparing the simple meal, she heard the sound she had been waiting for: that of Robert Campbell, bringing in the cows. Telling the children she'd be back in a minute, she slipped outside, into a yard which was already covered by a thin blanket of snow.

"Mr Campbell! Mr Campbell!" she called to him.

"Aye?" he turned slowly.

"The...the intruder has been here again. This very afternoon."

"Do you still think it's my mother?"

"I don't know what to think. But I feel very worried."

Quickly she explained to him what had happened.

"It's strange, all right. Who do you think it might be?"

"I don't know. Some tramp, I suppose."

"Usually they'd ask you if they could stay. They're not shy about that."

"No. I've never seen a tramp staying here, though."

"The Stewarts don't let them. That's why I don't think it's a tramp. They know the houses that will let them in, and stick to them, as a rule. Have you searched well?"

"Everywhere likely."

He scratched his head. The hot breath of the cows made wreaths of steam in the dark byre, lit by one weak oil lamp.

"It's odd, all right," he said.

"I know now it's not your mother," said Sally, to placate him, should he be feeling angry still.

"You do?"

"I know she'd never come out on a day like this."

"You're right. She's been crouched over the fire all day long. As far as I know," he added, politely. He felt he could afford to be polite again, now that his mother was no longer under suspicion.

"I'm worried," Sally said again. "I don't like to be here, alone, with the children. Anything could happen."

"Yes, I understand that. I understand, all right. But I don't think this intruder is going to harm you. He—or she—is not interested in meeting you, or anyone else, that I can see. But I can understand that you feel nervous. Maybe I should send your sister over to you, for company?"

"Why don't you do that!" said Sally, cheering up.

"I will," he promised. "I'll send her over immediately. And I will come over here early tomorrow morning, and I'll turn the place upside down. We'll find whoever it is then, do not fear. And tonight make sure you lock up everything. Bolt the doors and lock them, and fasten up all the windows. Nobody will get in. Not if they're human, anyway."

"No," said Sally, feeling shivery, and remembering all kinds of ghost stories she had heard at home in Donegal.

"Goodnight then, lass," said Robert Campbell. "I'll see you in the morning."

"Goodnight," said Sally, trudging slowly back across the yard.

21

Footprints in the Snow!

Sally decided to cook a special supper after all, since she was expecting Katie to come. But six o'clock came and went, and Katie did not appear.

"She's probably delayed by Mrs Campbell," said Sally to Emily, who was helping her and also looking forward to having a visitor. "Let's wait for a while."

Seven o'clock came. Sally went out to the gate and looked down the dark road, but there was no sign of Katie. She went back into the kitchen and gave the children more supper. She decided to wait until eight before having any herself. "If she hasn't come by eight, I'll stop hoping," she promised herself. "You never know nowadays what Katie will do, anyway." At eight, Katie had not appeared, and Sally thought she would wait for another half an hour, just in case. Although Katie had become a bit scatterbrained, she had been visiting Sally regularly for some time. And Robert Campbell was so completely reliable. He would never forget to send Katie over, once he had promised.

Sally began to feel very nervous: there was a horrible gnawing feeling in her stomach which she couldn't get rid of, and her head felt full of sharp objects: nails, or barbed wire, or something.

"Maybe she had to stay to put old Mrs Campbell to bed. Maybe she will come along later," suggested Emily, who could see how upset Sally was. Sally had never been this upset before, not since she came to the Stewarts.

"Maybe," said Sally. She felt like crying. "Why don't you go to bed now, dear. I'll put up Douglas and Jane."

When the children were safely in bed, she sat by the fire and stared into it. It was nine o'clock. Obviously Katie was not coming, for whatever reason. She hoped to goodness nothing had happened to her on the way over and banished all the thoughts that came into her head. She wished she could go out, walk over to Campbells' to find out what had gone wrong. But she couldn't. She couldn't risk leaving the children on their own.

"I've never felt so stuck!" she said, beating her fist against her forehead. "It's horrible, not being able to do a single thing to find out what's going on. It's the most horrible feeling of all, not knowing what is happening."

She decided to make another Christmas cake. She hadn't told the children that the first one had disappeared and didn't intend to tell them. Besides, she thought if she concentrated on doing something she would feel less worried and frightened. So she got out the bowl and the flour and all the ingredients, and made the cake.

The problem with this was that she had to wait until it was baked. Since it was already ten o'clock when she put the cake in the pot, this meant that she had to stay up until well after midnight. She knew she would not be able to sleep anyway, and so it was just as well to stay in the kitchen, keeping busy. She took out her library book and tried to read it. But she found she could not concentrate on the adventures of the only son, Charles Algernon Montgomery.

If his life had seemed unreal to her a few days ago, how much more unlikely did it seem now! It was not, however, because she was disbelieving that she could not get lost in the book. It was because she was petrified with fear. She sat, hunched up like Granny Campbell, listening to the deep silence of the house and starting at every sound. And that night the creaks were more numerous than usual, and every so often the scream of an animal from some distant field or wood made her heart beat madly and her mind fill with a heavy black terror. Once, she heard a cat cry horribly, and once, just about midnight, she thought she heard the kitchen door rattle. She remembered a frightening story Katie had told her, about a baby who had been killed by its mother, before it was baptised. She had wrapped the baby in a thin shawl and put it out near the sheepfold, where it died. The mother was a girl working on a farm, just like Sally. One night, around Christmas, everyone else on the farm went off to a dance. The girl didn't go, because she had nothing nice to wear, so she stayed at home, alone, keeping watch in the house. Around midnight she heard a scraping sound on the door. A high, thin, child's voice sang:

> *Mother mine, fold, fold,*
> *Do not fear the cold, cold!*
> *I will give you a shawl so thin*
> *For you to go dancing in!*

The girl knew who the voice belonged to. She became so frightened that she went completely mad.

The kitchen door rattled again. Sally clutched her heart, frightened out of her wits. She took the cake off the fire, although it was not really baked, and put it on the hearth. Then she crawled slowly up the stairs, jumping every time the floorboards creaked, and dived between the sheets. She felt a little safer, rolled up into a ball like a hedgehog, and eventually she fell asleep, while the wind howled around the creaking windows.

She woke up to the sound of bright living voices from the landing. A thin crack of light showed through the parting of the dark curtains, and threw a white glow, like a sheet, over the room. She stirred, yawned and sat up. Awake. Alive.

Morning.

Mornings are wonderful! she thought, jumping out of bed and running downstairs. No matter how terrible you feel at night, you feel better in the morning!

Emily and Douglas were already in the kitchen, the former poking at the embers of the fire, trying to get some heat out of it, because the air in the kitchen was ice-cold.

"Good morning, good morning!" said Sally. "I'll light that up now; you go and get on your very warmest clothes. Did you sleep well?"

She was all smiles as she heaped turf on the fire and stirred it into life. She prodded the cake with a fork: it seemed to be baked, and looked like most Christmas cakes do. She sang as she filled the kettle from the bucket of water on the kitchen dresser, and as she tested the porridge to see if it was done. Light-heartedly, she set the table for breakfast. They had survived the ordeal. It was morning. Soon, Robert Campbell would be here. He would tell her what had held Katie up: it was probably nothing at all. He would search for the intruder. He would find him. All would be well and she would never have to pass another night of fear and torment in this house.

She went to look out the window, to see if by any chance Campbell was already on his way. She drew back the curtains—and gasped. The whole countryside was deep in gleaming, brilliant snow. The fields, the houses, the trees, were all covered in it. In the quiet morning light they glittered and gleamed. Fairyland.

"Have you seen this, children?" called Sally. "Have you...?"

They couldn't hear her, so she ran upstairs to Emily's room, at the front of the house. The curtains had not been pulled back so she went to the window and drew them. "Just look!" she said in excitement. "Isn't it beautiful? Isn't it the most beautiful thing you have ever seen in...?"

And then she gasped once again. A deep gasp of shock. Because from her vantage place here at the upstairs window she could see something that had not been visible downstairs: a set of footprints, clearly visible in the virgin snow. They led from the cowhouse to the front door of the farm, and then away again to the farmgate and out on to the road.

"Robert Campbell's," said Sally to herself. "They must be Robert Campbell's."

But she knew they could not be. He had left long before the snow had become so deep, long before the snow had stopped falling. Whatever tracks he or she or the children had made had long been covered by the snowfall, which was three or four inches deep at least. These footprints had been made when it had stopped snowing, which must have been about midnight last night. Sally almost fainted, remembering that she had still been up, still in the kitchen, listening to the maker of those footprints, who had come silently to the kitchen door, tried it, and walked away again. Away from the farm!

No, Robert Campbell had not made the footprints. They were, in any case, too small to be his. He had very large feet, encased in heavy riding boots most of the time. These prints were not tiny, but they were not as large as his. They were medium-sized. They could be, they could be Katie's. Just about, although they seemed too big for her. Still, maybe in winter boots, borrowed winter boots...Anyway it was hard to tell the size exactly, from here. If the footprints were Katie's, where was she, in the cold, in the snow? If so, why didn't she come in, in the deep dark winter night?

I hope it wasn't her at the door at midnight, thought Sally. I hope it wasn't her I was frightened of, and didn't let in. What a coward I am!

22

The Intruder
Unmasked

"Look!" said Emily, when she came to the window. "Footprints! Whose are they?"

"I don't know, Emily," said Sally. "I don't know. I suppose they might be mine."

"Were you out last night in the snow?" asked Emily, in disbelief. "You weren't, were you? Are they...the ghost in the barn's?"

"Oh dear, Emily, I don't know," said Sally. "But if so she's not in the barn now. Let's go down and get some breakfast. And look," she said, pointing, "here comes Mr Campbell. Everything is going to be all right."

Robert Campbell came right up to the kitchen door, and knocked loudly. Sally ran and struggled to pull back the heavy bolt and unlock the door.

"No wonder your night visitor didn't get in," he said. "It's like the Bank of England here. And just as well too, I can see."

"Yes," said Sally. "I was up but I didn't hear anything last night. Still, you see for yourself how things are?"

"How so?"

Sally answered sharply, irritated at his slowness, or

pretended slowness: "You must have seen the footprints. They're not made by any one of us. Somebody came to the house last night and tried to get in."

"Did you see who it was?"

"No," she answered shortly. "I did not. I hope it wasn't Katie: she didn't come at all yesterday."

"Och no," he said. "Katie's at home. She wasn't able to get away: the old woman took a bad turn last night and wanted Katie to stay with her."

"Oh," said Sally.

"I'm sorry about that. You must have been worried. But how about this intruder, as you call him? I suppose we might as well look for him now."

"I think that's a good idea," said Sally. "Wait while I get my shawl."

Within minutes, she and Robert Campbell were following the footprints. They led out of the farm on to the road, and then took a turn to the right, in the direction of Ballygowl. Luckily the only other footprints on the road were Robert's, so it was easy to follow the intruder's marks along the road for about a quarter of a mile. Then they turned into a field, and petered out at a stack of hay which had been left, covered with a few old sacks, almost in the middle of it.

Robert and Sally exchanged a glance. What would they find behind the haystack? Not saying a word, for fear of giving warning to the intruder, if she or he were hiding, they glided across the brilliant field. Sally went around one side of the haystack and Robert Campbell the other. They met at the back of it, and both cried out in surprise; lying in the hay, half-covered in snow, was a young man, or rather a big boy. His feet and legs were covered in snow. The rest of his body was more or less buried in the hay. Robert pulled it away from his head and revealed the face of the boy from Stewarts' shop.

"Billy Stewart," he said, quietly. "Silly Billy, we always called him."

Sally was dumbfounded. Billy Stewart. The slow-witted boy from the grocer's shop in Ballygowl. What was he doing, hanging around the farm? "Is he…is he all right?" she asked, finally. The body was ominously still.

"He's alive, if that's what you mean," said Robert. "But he can't be very well. We'd better get him out of here and back to the house."

With considerable difficulty they pulled Billy to his feet. He was a large boy, and heavy, although he did have rather small feet. For a moment, he opened his eyes and mumbled something, but then they closed again.

"I doubt if he has the use of those legs. We're going to have to drag him," said Robert. Sally tried. But after a few minutes they had barely moved the heavy body at all, and it was obvious that they were not going to progress further.

"I'll go and get the horse," said Robert. "You'd better stay here with him. I don't think he'll give you any trouble."

Sally did not relish the thought but she had little choice. She waited in the cold field, trying to brush the snow from Billy's feet and rub some life into them. They were stiff and freezing like blocks of ice. She rubbed and rubbed, but it made no difference at all. However, it gave her something to do and she did not notice the passage of time until Robert returned, with his horse and, to her surprise, a large, neat sleigh. They managed to get Billy into the sleigh. Then Robert told her to hop in beside him, and he sat on the driver's seat and guided the horse back to the Stewarts' farm.

"Make a bed for him by the fire, can you do that?" Robert

asked, when they had reached the kitchen. Sally did as she was told, wondering what she would find herself doing next. Putting Billy into the bed and filling a hot water bottle, was the answer. He didn't wake at all while he was being moved from the sleigh to the kitchen, from the floor to the makeshift bed.

"I think he's got frostbite," said Robert. "I'm away to get the doctor and to tell his mother where he is. You won't have any trouble with him, even if he does come to, which I doubt. He's a harmless poor fool at the best of times."

Sally piled turf on the fire and stoked it up, so that the kitchen was soon warm and cosy. Billy Stewart lay in his bed by the fire, not stirring but breathing easily enough. Sally, although beginning to feel sorry for him, was relieved that he did not seem to be waking up. She hoped he was all right but she would prefer to have him as a sleeping guest until someone else was on the scene to help him. She was gratified to see, however, that colour was gradually returning to his face. She took this as a hopeful sign.

She and the children had breakfast, and tried to behave as if the ghost from the barn were not lying by their fireside thawing out and waiting to be examined by the doctor. They did their best to act as if nothing unusual was happening. After breakfast, Douglas and Jane went out to play in the yard, and, encouraged by Sally, built an enormous snowman. Sally and Emily worked in the kitchen, glancing from time to time at Billy. Both were relieved to see that his once livid face was nearly restored to a normal colour but they were also glad to note that he showed no sign of waking up.

At about eleven o'clock, there was another surprise for Sally: the postman arrived, bringing a letter addressed to her. It was in her mother's hand.

Dearest Sally,

Thank you very much for your letter. I am glad to hear that you are happy and doing well, as we are ourselves. I have made some money from my knitting, and the farm is doing nicely. The neighbours are very helpful. We miss you very much and wish you could be with us, especially now that it is Christmas. However, please be brave. Once Christmas is past you will not feel it till May and then we will be together again.

Janey misses you both a lot: she keeps asking when you are coming home, and if you will have sweets for her. I have managed to get her a new doll and a lot of sweets for her Christmas stocking. It won't be the same as having her sisters home, but it will make her happy enough, I hope.

Tell Katie I was asking for her. How is she? Is she getting on as well as you are? Have a happy Christmas. Love from all here,

Mother

When she read the letter, Sally could no longer restrain her feelings. She sat down at the kitchen table and cried and cried. It was such a great relief to have some word from Mother and from home. But the kind words in the letter, the very ink and paper, reminded her of how much she missed her family and her home. There was no one for her in Tyrone.

No one, that is, except Emily and Jane and Douglas and Robert Campbell and old Granny Campbell and now Billy Stewart from the shop...and the whole new life that she had become entangled in, almost against her will. She had only been here for a few months, but so much had happened that she felt it had been much longer. Ballygowl could never be home. But in a strange way she did feel at home here now. It was as if she had two homes.

She folded up the letter and stuck it in the pocket of her dress. At that moment, Robert Campbell and the doctor marched into the kitchen.

"There he is over there," said Robert.

"Aye aye, I can see that, not blind yet, you know," the doctor was puffing and blowing, looking, as always, like old pictures of the west wind after a heavy night's blowing.

"And how's Mary from Dungloe?" he said, winking and tweaking Sally's chin as he went by her, emitting a strong stench of ice and whiskey. "Or is it the Rose of Arranmore?"

Sally could not think of a suitably smart answer.

"Not happy?" asked Robert, as the doctor finally went about his business, much to everyone's relief. "I thought your worries would be over now that we caught yon ghost. Or was it witch?"

Sally was just not interested in jokes at the moment. She watched the doctor examining Billy.

"Have you been talking to his mother?" she asked after a while.

"Yes. She'll be over in the next hour or so. And then we'll take Billy home in my sleigh. I happen to be the only man in this parish who owns a sleigh. Makes me useful at times like this, said Robert."

"It surely does. But what's the explanation of Billy's behaviour? Why has he been here at all?"

"Och, she doesn't know. How could anyone know that, with someone like poor Billy? He's a bit strange as you know. He does odd things from time to time. Everyone around here knows that. There is no explanation. That's just the way he is."

"But..." This reasoning struck Sally as being unsatisfactory. "Is that all there is to it? Nobody is going to try to get to the bottom of it?"

"What is there to get at? He's not very bright, Billy. He takes odd notions. Probably he saw you at the shop buying sweeties or something. Perhaps he took a notion of you, who knows? He does things like that. He's not right in the head."

"Obviously not," said Sally, with irony which Robert Campbell failed to notice. She did feel sorry for Billy, up to a point. But it seemed wrong that nothing was going to be done about his behaviour, no attempt made to understand it or try to ensure that it wouldn't happen again.

"He's never violent," said Robert, reading her thoughts. "He would not harm a fly, Billy wouldn't. There really is no need to worry about him. And God knows he won't do much harm or good for a good wee while after this. If at all. How is the patient, doctor?"

"He'll be better before he's twice married, I shouldn't wonder," said the doctor. "A wee touch of frostbite on the right foot, but I don't think it'll have to come off. Not yet anyway. But what's a foot here or there, what? Any whiskey left over from the Christmas baking, Mary, what?"

"No," said Sally, firmly. She was finding the doctor tiresome today. Didn't he ever know when to stop? Anyway she didn't know where William Stewart kept his supply of whiskey. Probably he had drunk it all before he left. "Any more word from William Stewart to you, doctor?"

"Aye, aye," said the doctor, taken aback by her forthright refusal. "He'll be back today or tomorrow, earlier than expected. Everything is all right. I'd a note from him yesterday or the day before. The missus is well. As well as she'll ever be, anyway."

"Oh?" said Sally, raising her eyebrows questioningly.

"What do you mean, as well as she'll ever be?"

"No more nor less than I'm saying, Rosie. And now if you've no refreshment to offer me, I'll say good-day to you." He bowed deeply and headed for the door. Before leaving, he turned to Robert: "You can take the wee scut back to his mammy any time you like, Bob. He'll be better looked after at home, I have no doubt."

23

Happy Christmas!

Robert Campbell took Billy back to his mother, as the doctor had prescribed, and peace reigned in the Stewart farm for the rest of that day. The children played in the snow, and in the afternoon went down to the duck-pond which was thickly coated in ice and slid on it to their hearts' content. Sally cooked the tastiest meals she could muster up, and they drank raspberry cordial and ate biscuits and cakes for afternoon tea. It was the happiest day they had had in weeks.

The next one was even happier, at least for the Stewart children. It was Christmas Eve, the day all children and all grown-ups, who have not forgotten that they are big children, love. A bright sunny day, it was still cold enough to ensure that the snow lay undisturbed on the ground and the whole countryside looked like a Christmas card. There was even a fat robin on the window sill of the kitchen. Emily fed it crumbs.

While Douglas and Jane tumbled in the snow, Sally and Emily worked, making the house pretty, and making last-minute preparations for the day ahead. Robert Campbell came in the morning, as usual, and called in to tell them that he had delivered Billy Stewart safely and that he seemed to be getting better. He brought with him a large package from the Stewart shop. It was for Sally and the children, he said, as a small repayment to them for the unpleasantness they had suffered during the past week. Sally was surprised at this. She had thought the shop owners should make some apology to her and the children, but she hadn't really expected that they would. After all, she was the lowest of the low in their eyes: a poor servant girl from Donegal.

Like Emily and the two smaller children, she was very excited at the sight of the large parcel. With pleasure she pulled off the thick twine and unwrapped the brown paper that covered it. Inside was a box, containing tins of chocolates and biscuits, jars of jam, oranges and bananas, a bright red hat, which could only have been meant for Sally, some toys, and two books. Each of the items was pulled out and exclaimed over with shouts of joy by everyone. Sally put on her hat, which suited her beautifully, and Jane and Douglas played with the spinning tops they had got. For Emily there was a small silk shawl. She put it on over her pinafore and they all danced around with glee. When their excitement was subdued a little, they sat down and opened the smaller of the two boxes of chocolates, and shared them with Robert Campbell, who had witnessed the opening with a certain staid interest and who was quite willing to eat his share. He had a sweet tooth.

They were finishing the first layer when William Stewart walked into the kitchen.

"How do you do, Robert," he said, smiling rather warmly—for him. "Are you having a party? When the cat's away the mice will play."

Everyone jumped up. Sally took off her hat and Robert

swallowed his chocolate caramel whole. The children stopped playing with their tops and smiled at their father. But none of them ran over to him.

Then a second figure walked, slowly, into the room. It was Mrs Stewart, dressed, it seemed, in about a hundred layers of clothing, so that she looked like a pincushion. Underneath all the clothes she looked very thin and pale. But she smiled weakly and held out her arms. The children no longer restrained themselves but ran to her. For a moment they clung together. The mother and the children all cried, and Sally, watching them, felt her eyes fill with tears.

After the first emotional moments, Mrs Stewart sat down by the fire, and removed a few of her outer layers of clothes. The children gathered around her, plying her with chocolates and questions. She, in her turn, made certain enquiries, and was assured that they had been very well cared for, and had not caught colds, or missed days at school, or been in any way neglected. They did not bother to tell her about all their adventures. Even Douglas seemed to realise that it wasn't the time to do that.

Meanwhile, William Stewart sat with Robert and Sally, and received their account of the past weeks. The only problem, Sally said, had been the intruder, and that had been solved. William Stewart's eyes looked angry while he listened to the story. But he congratulated Sally on her courage and thanked Robert for all the help he had given in the affair.

"Still, they should not have been left alone here," he said, looking hard at his neighbour. "Could you not have stayed here with them, when you heard about it?"

"No," said Robert. "I could not leave the old woman on her own."

"Didn't she have the girl?"

"Och, well, it's not the same thing. She's just a wee one, Katie. Not as sensible as Sally here at all."

Sally felt surprised, hearing this said. Of course she realised that she was older than Katie and had behaved in a more grown-up way than her ever since she had come to Ballygowl. Katie had seemed to become so childish, as soon as she left home! Still, it was funny to hear an adult comment on her own sense. Sally had never once in her whole life in Donegal been described as sensible. That was the last thing her mother or any of her friends or neighbours had thought her. Scatterbrain Sally.

Sensible. Grown-up. A head on her shoulders.

She was not sure if she liked being thought of in these terms. She hadn't particularly wanted to be grown-up. But she hadn't had much choice. And now here she was, not scatterbrained and childish any more, but sensible and mature. Would she be different, if she were at home, she wondered? Would she ever be her old silly self again?

She left the kitchen and went upstairs to her room, where she lay on the bed and buried her head in the pillow. She did not cry but she was struck by a deep feeling of emptiness. Everything was going to change again now, and probably for the worse. The holiday was over. It was true, what Mr Stewart had said. When the cat's away the mice will play. Sally and the children would have had a marvellous time, playing at Christmas. What fun it would have been, hiding the presents she had got for the children, cooking their Christmas dinner, trying to make things pleasant and amusing for them. She knew they were glad to be reunited with their parents. But she wondered if they would have as much fun tomorrow as they would have if the parents had stayed away. What a pity they had had to come home just now. Could they not have waited for a few more days, until

Christmas was out of the way?

Sally was aroused from her sad thoughts by a knock at the door. She sat up, patted her hair and said, "Come in." It was William Stewart.

"You are upset?" he asked, in his stiff manner.

"A little," said Sally.

"It is natural. You have had a difficult time and a great deal of trouble. I want to thank you for looking after my family so well. I can see that they have been cared for better than I could have hoped."

"Thank you," said Sally, in a small voice.

"I would like to thank you in some more practical way, and have been trying to think of one. I thought, more money. But Robert Campbell has another suggestion."

"Oh?" said Sally. More money would have been useful. It sounded like a good idea to her.

"Yes. He thinks that I should send you home for Christmas. Your sister can go too, of course."

Sally could not believe her ears.

"Home? Home to...home?"

"Home to Donegal. You may not get there tonight, but it should be possible to arrive sometime tomorrow. Christmas Day. There is a trap waiting outside, the one we came in. The train for Letterkenny leaves Ballygowl in an hour's time. I'll give you some money and you will be able to get a ride from there."

Sally could think of absolutely nothing to say. She did not know what he was talking about. Was she leaving for good? Was she being sacked? Or what?

"I think a week's holiday might be in order. Then I would expect you to return here, and finish your term according to the contract. Of course, if you do not do that, you forfeit your wages."

Of course! The contract was the contract!

"Does that idea appeal to you, Sally?"

"Yes, it appeals to me. Thank you, I think it's a very good idea."

"In that case, you had better pack your bag. Here is a pound, which should be more than you need for your travel expenses. You can leave here in ten minutes and we'll see you again on the second of January. The day after New Year's Day," he added, in case Sally did not know when the second of January was.

"I know," she said. "Thanks very much. I'll be down in a minute."

She changed into her Sunday dress and boots and wrapped the rest of her belongings, including some of the presents from Stewarts' shop, in her old red shawl. That did not take long. Then she ran downstairs and kissed the children goodbye. They cried and were sorry to see her go, but she comforted them with the promise of her speedy return. Just as she stepped into the trap Emily cried, "Stop! Wait a minute!" She dashed into the house and returned a few seconds later with a small, gaily wrapped parcel.

"Your Christmas box!" she said to Sally. "You're not to open it until tomorrow. When we're opening ours!"

"I'll be thinking of you then," said Sally, kissing her again, and thinking that she had grown extremely fond of all the Stewart children over the past weeks. Just as she had become fond of life in Ballygowl and was beginning to think of it as a place where she belonged and could be happy.

The driver whipped the horses and they began to walk slowly towards the gate. Sally waved a last goodbye. The trap left the farmyard and on the road, covered with hard-packed snow, the horses broke into a smart, steady trot.

Clip-clop, clip-clop, went their feet, ringing against the freezing ground. At the Campbells' cottage they stopped and collected Katie, who could not believe her good luck. The two girls sat arm-in-arm in the trap, their eyes sparkling like stars. They did not say a word, after the first greetings and explanations were over. They were much too emotional to speak. Home. They were going home for Christmas. Tomorrow they would be sitting at their own fireside, eating goose and plum pudding with their mother, playing with little Janey. During the coming week they would see all their friends: Maura, Miss Lynch. Manus, maybe, with a bit of luck. Now that this was going to happen, they were at last able to admit to themselves how much they wanted it. They were able to let themselves feel everything that was in their hearts. And what they felt was pure joy.

Glossary
of Folklife and Historical Terms

Folklife

Crane — an iron crane hanging over the fire, from which a pot or kettle could be hung

Harning stand — an iron stand which supported a cake of bread as it baked in front of the fire

Hiring fair — fair or market at which people offered themselves for hire as servants or labourers

Meitheal — group of people who gathered together to perform some big agricultural task, such as harvesting or thrashing, in cooperation

Pot-oven — a pot, suspended over the fire, which was used instead of an oven. Closed ovens were very uncommon in Irish country houses.

Wake — the night before a funeral, when the family and friends of the bereaved gathered in his or her house to stay awake with the corpse and to have a party

Wean — child

History

Gladstone — William Gladstone, leader of the Liberal Party at Westminster, was Prime Minister of England, on and off, from 1868 to 1894

Home Rule — a limited form of self-government by Ireland. This was Parnell's main political goal.

Land Acts — from the 1870s until the beginning of the twentieth century, a series of land acts were passed by the English parliament which improved the conditions of Irish tenant farmers. For instance, the Ashbourne Act of 1885 provided loans which enabled tenants to buy out the land they were renting from landlords. This is the act which is referred to in this book. In practice, it took a long time before all tenants could benefit from the provisions of the act.

Land League	founded in 1879 to campaign for the improvement of conditions on the land
Orange Lodge	a branch of the Orange Order, founded in 1795 in Armagh and still in existence. It represents the Protestant people of Ulster who have a strong wish to remain linked to Great Britain. In the nineteenth century, Orangemen were opposed to ideas such as Home Rule for Ireland, or any form of Irish independence.
Katharine O'Shea	separated from her husband, Captain O'Shea, Katharine O'Shea met Parnell in 1880. They fell in love. She was divorced in November 1890, the year in which this novel is set, and married Parnell in June 1891. The divorce caused a great scandal which ended Parnell's political career. He died in October 1891, in Katharine's arms.
Charles Stewart Parnell	"the uncrowned King of Ireland." He was born in Avondale, Co Wicklow in 1846. In 1875 he was elected a Member of Parliament and in 1880 he became leader of the Irish Party at Westminster. He was a very successful and inspiring politician. He brought about many reforms which benefited Irish tenants, and was campaigning with some success for Home Rule when his career and life ended in 1891.

Also by Poolbeg

Blaeberry Sunday

By

Elizabeth O'Hara

*That summer had changed the
course of her life for ever:
"Was every little thing that happened
as significant as every other little
thing in shaping the course of
a person's life?"*

The summer leading up to Blaeberry Sunday
—the festival of Lughnísí—in 1893 was the
hottest and driest anyone in Donegal had
ever experienced. Determined not to remain a
hired girl for the rest of her days, Sally returns
to Glenbra only to witness an eviction, death,
and the courtship of her mother and Packy
Doherty, a local farmer. Nothing, however, is
quite so devastating as her love for Manus
McLoughlin and the events preceding that
fateful Blaeberry Sunday.

Also by Poolbeg

Penny-farthing Sally

by

Elizabeth O'Hara

Penny-farthing Sally completes the award winning trilogy about Sally Gallagher which began with *The Hiring Fair* and *Blaeberry Sunday*.

Sally is employed as a governess at the home of the Erikson family in Dublin. Through the Eriksons she encounters many famous people, including WB Yeats and Douglas Hyde, and experiences the hectic, exciting life of Dublin – a city of contrasts – at the turn of the century.

Sally learns to ride a bicycle, sees the first motor cars and attends the first performance of Yeats' play, *The Countess Kathleen*. She also goes to meetings of the Gaelic League where she meets new friends, Ethel and Thomas.

Penny-farthing Sally evokes the excitement and energy of Dublin at the dawn of the twentieth century – it is also the sensitive and tender story of a girl at the dawn of adulthood. Change is sweeping through Ireland – revolution and romance are in the air!